ELVEN CHAOS

BATHED IN DRAGON'S BLOOD
BOOK 2

AL K. LINE

Small Job

"Do not," I warned, "eat any of these maniacs. I don't want you turning into an old hag and running around the house cackling."

Tali turned her head on thick, sinewy neck muscles and locked her always mesmerizing eyes on mine. "Looked like tasty treat," she hissed, glancing at the rundown shack and sniffing deeply. "Can have little taste?" she pleaded. "Need old lady bones to clean teeth. Is good for Tali."

"No, absolutely not. If you want to clean them, get a toothbrush. Do dragons even get plaque?" I mused.

"Tali's teeth always clean and sparkling." She opened her mouth, revealing pristine, razor-sharp weapons, the acrid scent of sulfur strong. It was an aroma I adored, just like I adored my dragon companion. Flames danced at the back of her throat, another indication Tali was keen to hunt.

A babbling, mad old crone sped from the house and ran, naked, into the woods, arms waving wildly. We let the filthy, wretched creature go; we'd catch up with her easily enough.

Tali's head snapped back around to me and I watched as tiny flecks of silver danced across the purple iris and deep red flickered for an instant in the orange sclera. A warning that her bloodlust was rising.

"But if you help me out, and promise not to feed on any of these disgusting abominations, I might have a treat for you when we get home."

"Is cheese? Cheddar?"

"No," I admitted, wishing it was. Why couldn't a guy get decent cheese nowadays? It was a crime, a perversion of our supposed "modern" world.

"Is what?"

"What?" I asked, losing my train of thought.

"What is?" Tali tried again, but now I was truly flummoxed.

"You need to practice your language," I admonished, changing tack and going over old ground. "When you ask a question, you should say, 'What is it?' not 'Is what?' Otherwise, things get confusing."

"Are confused? Is right way of speaking?" she asked, angling her beautiful, powerful head to the side. I got another hit of tangy sulfur as she snorted her amusement.

"Ah, you're messing with me," I laughed, then frowned when she didn't so much as bat an eyelid.

Nava sighed in pleasure as he lowered his leg from where he'd been peeing against a tree. "That's better," he grinned, the default setting for my painted dog companion of many years.

"Oh, good. I'm so happy for you," I grumbled. "Think we can actually get on with what we're here for now? You're the one who wanted to come, and all we've done is wait while you mark territory that isn't yours."

"I didn't want to miss out," he said as he padded over to us. "And besides, Charles said this was an emergency."

"It is. I could do without this so close to the elven chaos I'm sure will happen soon enough, but we can't let this small nest of insane Necros carry on like this. Everyone good?"

"Tali is good."

I studied Tali for a moment, then asked, "Do you know what I mean by that?"

"Is when behave well," she said proudly. "When do right thing. Tali do right thing at all times."

"So wrong," smirked Nava, shaking his head.

"I'll explain when we get home, Tali. For now, everyone just stick to the plan and this will be over soon enough."

"Famous last words," sniggered Nava, tail wagging.

I let the whispers I'd used to keep us from being heard fade away as Tali's impressive form materialized so others could see her. As we'd planned, Nava fed on the protective wards around the perimeter of this small nest's compound and began to change into something almost demonic. His wiry body became engorged with misshapen muscle, his head doubled, then tripled, in size, losing focus as it seemed to encompass the world as he once again bit into the impressive wards and devoured the magic.

He stumbled once, regained his footing, and snarled as he sprang from the cover of the trees and into the weed-infested clearing.

Tali thundered forward, her newly enlarged frame smashing spindly trees aside with a crack, then was airborne the moment she was clear.

I chased after them both, knowing I had scant minutes to get the prisoners out, assuming they were still alive, before it was game over when the sun began to rise.

The door to the ancient wooden house slammed open and an emaciated wizard wearing nothing but a filthy loin cloth, staff in hand, emerged. His eyes opened wide in shock as he spied me. Nava darted across my path, already chasing down the witch who'd run off earlier. The dark wizard lifted his staff, reflexes at odds with his appearance. The early morning, cool air hissed as he gathered his whispers then shot a blast of searing white energy right at my head.

Rather than ducking, I hefted Ziggy, my magical weapon of choice and even more of a constant companion than my two best friends, and let the broad wooden club absorb the energy and boost my own magic. Without missing a step, I surged forward and charged the shocked old man aside then continued into the hovel.

The smell, rather than the insane amount of clutter, caused me to grind to a halt, gagging. Flies buzzed around rotten food littering the floor, cat feces and worse was piled everywhere, and, most disgusting of all, several decomposing body parts hung from hooks above a shrine to some unholy creature these twisted fucks were enamored with.

More than enamored. They were followers of Malgog. His acolytes wallowed in their own filth, reveled in depravity and degradation of not only themselves but their victims. Hoarders, madmen, souls lost to dark magic and even darker practice, those that followed Malgog's path were the worst humanity had to offer.

Whispers began to creep insidiously into my head, so I spun and stormed back to the filth-encrusted man prone on his back by the door. As he redoubled his magical efforts and I felt the beginnings of their idol stir, reaching out to me from behind a weakening veil, I swung Ziggy, letting his form change into a sword, and ran though the man's eye, into his skull, and twisted. The body convulsed, then was still. With a grunt, I yanked Ziggy out and waded through the clutter, kicking aside broken furniture, avoiding the festering piles of rags, and holding back a threatening retch as a swarm of rats darted from the chest cavity of a half-rotten, headless male torso.

With sunrise almost upon us, I knew I had no time, and that Tali would play her part the moment I sent word, so I skidded through the foul living room, down a hallway with stained wallpaper hanging in strips, and into the room at the back of the house that I presumed they called a kitchen.

Two girls were shackled by chains hanging from the bowing, mold-covered ceiling. Neither could have been more than fifteen. Their torn clothes were filthy, bodies emaciated. They pleaded with desperate eyes and muffled cries from beneath their gags as I blasted into the room, scanning for the rest of the nest.

Two old, gray-haired women and one bald, beyond obese man were standing beside a sink overflowing with filthy water and a mountain of dishes and pans, greedily eating their breakfast with a faraway look in their eyes. They hadn't had a chance to even react as I'd stormed through the house so fast. The man clutched a dripping friend egg sandwich in fingers coated with yellow yolk, hand halfway to his mouth. His pale, bare torso was covered in tattoos of magical marks with numerous fresh incisions stitched together inexpertly. They offered their suffering gladly to the one they worshiped. Their stench was almost unbearable.

Ziggy flashed into a spear as I flung him at the man who dropped his meal and grabbed for his staff. Too late, the sleek metal pierced his hairy hide and found his heart. He choked on his half-chewed mouthful of food as he slumped to the tacky linoleum.

The witches were faster to react, and as I lunged for Ziggy, willing him to lengthen so I managed to grab hold and yank him free, they shot out their hands as whispers turned the cloying, humid room into a black pit.

My partial elven ancestry and Necro nature meant I saw better than most in the dark, but clearly not as well as these two as they worshiped a creature from the lightless places. Whispers whipped around my body, tightening their hold, my breathing already difficult. Ziggy sliced through the worst of it, breaking the witches' focus, then I was free.

Light returned, and I hacked roughly at the pair, knowing the time was almost upon us. In their enfeebled state, and certainly no warriors, they succumbed to my bloodlust easily enough. Once both were dispatched, I dashed over to the two girls and fumbled with the bindings holding their hands behind their backs. Freeing the knots with a slice from the dagger, I grabbed the terrified girls and led them quickly back the way I'd come, having to almost drag them when they froze in horror at the sight of the wizard at the front door.

Outside, I guided them away as fast as I could, but their legs were unstable and both kept stumbling. As we rushed for the trees, I turned and felt for Tali's presence.

Do it now, I called to her. *We're nearly out of time.*

Tali will buuurn, she hissed as she appeared above the shack, resplendent as the first of the sun's rays glinted off her shimmering green scales. The immortal dragon belched a steady stream of tight flame at the roof as she swept by. Thankfully, the two girls were facing the other way, and then Tali was gone, her body invisible once more.

"What... what happened?" stammered the dark-skinned girl as tears streamed down her face.

"They were about to sacrifice you. They do it at true dawn. We only had a minute left," I explained, thinking it best to tell them the truth. I'd had enough of lies and deception lately, and couldn't bring myself to pretend this was anything but life-threatening.

"You saved us! You really did!" She collapsed into the weeds, dragging her shrieking friend with her.

"Thank you so much," the small brown-haired girl stammered, her words slipping because of her split tongue.

"My pleasure. And they won't be doing this to anyone else. Look." I helped them both to their feet and we turned to witness the roof of the shack collapse inward. The entire structure went up with a *whoosh* as something flammable caught, sending bits of wood and decades of hoarding flying in every direction.

We jumped back as the shockwave hit, then watched, mesmerized, as the nest burned.

"How could they do this to us?" the petite girl sobbed, hugging her friend tight. "They beat us and made fun of us and kept us in that disgusting kitchen without food for days. They've done it before you know? To others."

"I know. We heard about it, and as soon as we could, we came to get you. Your parents will be so relieved."

Nava stumbled over, face bloodied, but thankfully back to his regular size. The girls recoiled, gripping each other, and me, tight.

"It's a wild dog! It's going to eat us."

"He's my friend," I soothed. "Don't be afraid. Nava here is a very good boy, aren't you?" I said, winking, knowing he hated doggie talk. "Would you like to stroke him? He's got very nice fur. Look at the patches. It's wiry, but soft too."

"I've heard of painted dogs," said the brave, slightly older girl. "Saw them online. They're from Africa," she declared proudly, seemingly having forgotten about the trouble they'd just been in.

And to some degree they had. I let my gentle whispers shroud them in a bubble of dreamy calm, easing their elevated stress levels somewhat, but not taking away the memory from them. I would never do that. I'd had a memory taken, and the consequences had been dire. I remembered little of my parents because the whispers had stolen them from me.

"He's so cute," smiled the younger girl.

"Be a good boy and let the girls stroke you, Nava," I said, beaming.

"If I must," he grumbled, then eased forward and bowed his head.

Both girls reached out and stroked his back, then giggled as they played with his large, curved ears.

"You overdid it with the whispers," noted Nava as he moved away and shook himself out.

"I think you might be right. They shouldn't be this relaxed."

"What was that?" asked the dark girl.

"Oh, just talking to Nava."

"He sounds funny. His barks and whines make it seem like he's talking."

"I know. Funny, right?" I beamed at the two girls, then told them, "Let's get you home."

They nodded eagerly, then a darkness fell over them as my whispers faded away and the true extent of the horror they'd just endured came rushing back in.

"Oh my god, oh my god," blubbered one.

"They were going to kill us. Sacrifice us," screamed the other.

"Maybe you should have let the whispers take away the memory," said Nava, always wise.

I nodded to him, but I knew I was right not to mess with their heads. There was no knowing what else would be taken from them, and I didn't feel I had the right to interfere in their mental development.

But there was something I had to do.

Get them home.

"Here, both of you take a drink. Your lips are cracked and you can hardly speak properly. Just a few sips. You aren't used to it and it will make you sick otherwise."

They nodded mutely as I handed them a flask.

"So thirsty," gasped the brown-haired girl, then took a deep drink before handing it to the other. She took several tentative gulps, then passed the flask back to me.

"Better?" I asked with a smile, well aware I was a rather scary sight with Ziggy still clutched in my hand and blood splattered across my face and clothes.

"Much. Can we go home now?"

"Sure. Now look, I need to tell you both something. Don't be scared, but I put a little something in the water. It will help you relax. To sleep. When you wake up, I promise you will be home and this will seem like a bad dream. But I'm trusting you both to never describe me to anyone. I'm not the police. I work for a super-secret organization who help people who have been attacked by bad people like they were. You understand?"

"Course we do. We're Necro too. We get how this works. You gave us a potion so you can get us home without us knowing any more details. We aren't dumb."

"Great, that's great!" I sighed, beyond relieved. "Keep my name and Nava's out of this. Even to your parents. Explain what happened, but no descriptions, and certainly no names."

"We don't even know your name anyway."

I considered this briefly, then said, "I'm Kifo."

"Thank you, Kifo."

With a nod, I asked, "We good?"

"We're good," they both agreed, yawning. Then they collapsed, and would remain asleep long enough for the trip.

"Tali, you can come help now," I called.

My beautiful, impressive dragon materialized beside us, her scales reflecting orange hues from the burning building.

"Tali hid well," she said, proud as always of her abilities.

"You did. And thank you. Those foul people won't be causing any more problems. Nava, did you get the woman and the rest?" I asked.

"Of course. They're dead. But they tasted disgusting. What were these people?"

"Sick, twisted, and degenerate. They've been at this for years and years, but nobody has ever been able to track them down. Charles got some intel, apparently, and here we are. Who knows how many they have sacrificed to that thing they worshiped?"

"Too many."

"People are strange," said Tali, studying the sleeping girls.

"They sure are. These witches and wizards wallowed in everything that's wrong with humanity, but now they're gone. Let's get these two innocents home."

I loaded them both onto Tali's back as carefully as I could, no easy feat, then Nava hopped up reluctantly and I got myself comfortable.

Tali spread her wings and dashed through the clearing, then we were airborne. We circled the ruined compound once, just to be sure our work was done, then Tali drifted away. Smoke rose into the early dawn as we headed east to return the children to their families.

It was mere minutes before we arrived at a quiet farm many miles away, and landed with Tali cloaking her presence and therefore ours while we were in contact with her. I lay the girls on the ground as they began to stir, the potion I'd given them already wearing off. They were on their own now, and would recognize where they were, so our work was done.

With a grunt of satisfaction, we left, and made our way home.

The moment we arrived, Nava raced off to roll around in the grass to get the stench of the morning off. Adept at devouring wards and using other Necro's magic to his advantage, it always exhausted him, so I knew he'd want to be alone once satisfied he was clean.

I turned to Tali and put my hand to her lowered snout, marveling at her fine dragon features, lost in her mesmerizing eyes. Our bond deepened, a spiritual connection, and I felt the power between us.

Tali feels it too.

Are you reading my mind?

Not mind. Energy. Feel Kifo's love. Bond. Tali feels the same. Are bonded.

We are. Forever.

As she had done so many times since she fed from the witch's blood, Tali suddenly changed into the form of an intoxicating woman. Only the peculiar eyes remained that of the dragon.

I reached out and tentatively stroked her cheek, feeling our bond deeper than ever, her power over me disconcerting. Static ran up my arm, then it was as if it shot straight into my heart, and I gasped at the depth of the emotion I felt for her.

"You're so beautiful. Does it hurt still?"

"Is strange being woman. Feel whole but not whole. Different but same," she said, frowning as she studied her hands.

"We need to keep practicing if we're going to help Shi get what he wants."

"Will save friend. Save family. Will be whole when bathes in elf water?"

"That's what he says. If he bathes in the waters of Elinor, it will take away his shape-shifting problem and he won't have to run from things like he has his whole life. Like he did from me and Charles. But we need you to be a woman in the elven homeworld, at least part of the time."

"Am practicing lots. Am best at being woman. Look pretty. But is tiring. Feel sleepy."

"Then sleep. Rest. You did fine work this morning."

Tali stared into my eyes for the longest time, then purred, "Will let Tali share bed with Kifo?" It wasn't the first time she'd asked.

"We already discussed this," I gulped, trying to avoid admiring her fine figure, her perfect, pale skin, and her long, silver blond hair that hung down past her breasts.

Kifo not want to mate? she asked directly into my mind.

You know it isn't as simple as that. You've only been able to become a woman recently, and you don't understand what it means. I don't even know if I do, I admitted, feeling hot, my thoughts churning.

Feel heat in Kifo. Kifo wants. And Tali wants. Is simple.

"Nothing about this life is simple," I told her. "We have too much going on for us to even think about what you becoming a woman means. Let's focus on training you, and don't forget what we're doing later on. You think you will be up for it?"

Tali shifted back into dragon form and craned her neck forward until her nostrils touched my nose.

Tali is dragon. Do anything. She snorted, sulfur and something more subtle, more intoxicating, stirring my senses. The scent of woman. Her scent. I hadn't been able to get it out of my system since the first time she shifted, and it left me gasping.

"You can do anything," I agreed. "But some things aren't meant to be."

She snorted again, then spoke. The words ringing in my ears as she curled up and closed her eyes.

Some things are meant to be. Are inevitable.

Maybe they were. But that didn't always make them right.

Urgent Assistance

Mai was in one of his moods, probably because my clothes smelled of smoke and were somewhat bloodied. Wanting peace and quiet, and the chance to relax before Charles arrived, I took a mundane mug of coffee—I was out of the good stuff, or Mai had hidden it, which he sometimes did—outside and sat in the shade beneath an oak at the edge of my cleared compound. The heat was already getting up, and the humidity along with it. What I wouldn't give for the weather of old. I always marveled at the stories Charles told, even of when I was a boy, when we would have cool summers and it would rain almost every single day. It seemed almost magical, and quite unbelievable, that England used to be a wet and mostly cloudy country. I couldn't even imagine such a thing.

I got to have about three sips before my phone rang. "Hello?"

"Kifo, is that you?" asked a garbled voice.

"Who's this?"

"Arch."

"You're calling me? What's up? We've never spoken on the phone before. You okay? Has something happened to Charles?"

"No, at least I don't think so. That's why I'm calling. I can't get hold of him. There has been a, er, mishap, and I can't reach him. It's a matter of some urgency. Meaning, get yourself here as soon as possible. Bring the wolf. We might need him." Arch hung up.

"What the hell was that about?" I muttered. Arch and I had never been what you'd call buddies. In fact, he didn't have friends, and for the most part neither did I. It suited him and it suited me. I was happier when it was me, Nava, Tali, and Mai. Anyone else and life always got incredibly complicated. Plus, assassins weren't meant to have friends. Danger always lurked, or I was running straight towards it, and who wants to risk their friends? And as for family? Well, that's a different matter, as I had discovered recently.

What was I meant to do? Just go racing off to London on what would undoubtedly be a dumb pretense and he just wanted me to pick up a book or some such crap? But maybe not. We hardly ever spoke, he never went out for more than a few minutes, and his agoraphobia had got much more severe in recent years. But being such a proud man, he never, ever asked for a favor. And where was Charles?

My phone rang again. I couldn't believe how strong the signal was. The powers-that-be must have been in a good mood and weren't limiting everyone's reception for a change, although my internet had been intermittent for weeks now.

"Just so you know, this is very important. If you don't get here quickly, something terrible will happen."

"I can't get there that quick!"

"You can, and you will. If you want my help with your little expedition, then this is your final warning. There are people inside the house. Or, um, maybe not people, but intruders. I'm going to have to—"

The line went dead. My signal was gone.

"Bollocks!"

I gulped the scalding, bitter coffee with a curse and a grimace, then raced towards the house, shouting as I went. "Tali, no time for resting. We have to go to London." As she roused from her slumber, I yanked open the front door and stomped inside.

"Are you insane? Have you lost what little sense you had? Do you believe yourself to be a filthy pig on a farm, or are you still a human being?" screeched Mai, boot radar on full alert as he dashed from the broom cupboard where he liked to nap when he wasn't working, or endlessly re-arranging the many cloths and bottles of sprays.

"Sorry, but this is an emergency," I whimpered, sliding to a halt when his face turned puce as he noted the mud marks on the otherwise spotless floorboards.

"There is nothing that could warrant such hostile behavior. Take your boots off. Now!" he demanded, brandishing his duster like a deadly weapon, already dashing for the broom cupboard.

"What's all the fuss?" asked Shi—my hopefully temporary house guest—as he exited the spare bedroom with a yawn then scratched in places best scratched in private.

"Arch just called and said we have to get there, right now. There's something happening, intruders he said, and it would jeopardize our entire mission. We need to go. Now!"

"Shoo, shoo." Mai ushered me towards the front door, cloths, sprays, and who knew what else poking out of his green housecoat pockets, duster still clenched in his hand just in case.

"Mai, this is important," I snapped, holding my ground halfway to the door as he shoved at my knees. I slid backwards—he was stronger than he looked—which caused him to panic as the floor was getting dirtier, so with one hand on a spray bottle, the other on me, he both pushed and cleaned simultaneously.

I pleaded to Shi, my father, which was still a beyond weird thing to accept, with my eyes as he watched, amused, clearly not going to help.

"Mai knows what is important, and keeping a clean house is the most important. You boys and your silly games," he tutted. "Whatever is wrong with you lately?"

"He's very naughty," agreed Shi as he returned from the kitchen, munching on cold toast.

Mai beamed, glad to have backup, then went apoplectic. "Where's your plate? Have you no manners? Are you a beast of the field? Do you moo? Respectable people use plates. They do not," he lectured, "drop crumbs over floors kept clean by poor house gnomes. Outside, both of you. I can't get a moment's rest in this filthy hovel. Shame on you both."

Shi sauntered over with a smile, but it soon got wiped off his face when Mai launched at him, nabbed his half-eaten toast, and flung it towards the opening front door. It spun as it flew outside, and as I chuckled then turned to leave, I gawped as Nava came from nowhere, sprang, and caught then devoured the snack before landing and grinning at me.

I laughed, then clapped and said, "Nice moves. Look, we have to go. Keep an eye on things here. We need to go on Tali, and morph, so just guard the house. If anything happens, you know what to do."

"Kill them," Nava growled knowingly.

"Yeah, and don't make them breakfast first. Damn, what a morning."

We turned as Shi catapulted through the open front door. Mai wagged his feather duster in warning, then slammed the door shut—he would never let me leave it open, even if there was a nice cool breeze, as he believed dust could infiltrate and possibly even attack.

Shi landed on all fours, reflexes sharp, then stood and shook himself out like a wet dog. "Damn, he's feisty this morning. What's got into him?"

"He wasn't happy about my clothes being bloodied and stinking of smoke. Nice lie-in while we worked?"

"Yeah," he yawned. "But hey, man, I offered to come and help. You said no. What was I supposed to do?"

"Get up early to make us breakfast, then worry about us until we got home safely?" I offered.

Shi grinned. "No son of mine could be beaten by a small nest of decrepit monster-worshipers. How'd it go? You get the kids out in time?"

"We did. It was foul in there. The poor things were terrified and in a bad way. But we took them home. Tali burned the place down."

"Good riddance," grunted Shi.

"I'm not sure I like you calling me son," I said, meeting his eyes.

"Too soon?"

"A little. I'm still really pissed off with you and Charles about the whole thing. You both told so many lies, manipulated me, and had me doing things without knowing why. Charles has always been like that, but you? It wasn't a nice feeling to be pressed into helping without knowing the facts."

"I'm sorry, I really am. I wish I could have told you who I was and how I knew Charles, but I knew it would blow the whole thing wide open before it even began. And I'm sorry I haven't been around for you. You understand why, right? That I didn't want to put you at risk with me shape-shifting? I thought I was doing the right thing. Then when the elves finally came, well, it was game on. If I'd tried to explain it all, what then?"

"I don't know," I replied honestly.

"And that's fair enough. It's a lot to process. But I feel terrible about the secrets. You not knowing why we couldn't go get Charles the moment he was taken. He needed time, an opportunity, and it was a big risk. But whatever else Charles might be, he's family. Both of ours. He did this for me, and you did it for him. Maybe it was wrong to put you in such danger, but I figured you'd be up for it and maybe even be glad you helped your family once you knew what the deal was. Was I wrong?"

"No, you were right. But I get enough spook bullshit from Charles. I don't want my own father acting that way too. It'll take time, but I'm getting used to having you in my life. I wish I could remember what life was like before..."

"Before I turned into a wolf-man and killed your mother? Yeah, me too, mate, me too. Please forgive me?"

"For what?"

"For killing her. I can't forgive myself, never, but maybe you can?"

"I do. Of course. It wasn't your fault. You did all you could to stop it, to stay away, but it still got you. We're Necros, creatures of magic and madness, and we know it's the risk we take by being what we are. Magic, whispers, Necronotes from who knows where, forced to kill each other, it's a mad world and I understand that. So, yes, I forgive you. Dad."

Shi beamed, and skipped the distance between us and wrapped his strong arms around me. For a moment, I felt like a young boy safe in his father's arms. But I was a grown man, an assassin, with more deaths to my name than I could recall. I was corrupt, and a hard man, but still. It felt nice.

We broke with a hearty slap of the shoulders like men do, then Shi adjusted the sword strapped to his back, hitched up his jeans, and said, "Now, I thought you said this was urgent? What are we doing hanging around here getting soppy?"

"Tali is waiting," she hissed.

Shi and I jumped, then turned to find her head looming over us, the tang of sulfur and that other more intoxicating aroma strong. Steam escaped from her nostrils as her eyes shone with something akin to mirth.

"Have you been polishing your horns?" asked Shi. "They look so shiny and really go with your eyes."

"Tali not need to polish. Am great dragon and always clean. Horns grow more. Curve right back now. Can hold them when ride on Tali. Saw reflection in glass, so know. Look very big."

"You are a very impressive dragon," I told her, winking at Shi who groaned. "What's wrong?"

"I just remembered how much I hate flying. No offense, Tali."

"Flying is wonderful thing. Best. Must go?"

"Yes, we must. I bet it's some nonsense, but Arch isn't the kind of person to mess around. And besides, Shi needs the practice flying, and Tali, you need to learn how to go easy on us so it isn't as terrifying."

"Not be scared. Tali will protect delicate men."

"Gee, thanks," laughed Shi.

With plenty of reasons to dawdle, but none that would sit well with Arch, I settled myself into the saddle at the base of Tali's neck that had formed over the years as our bond grew, gripped the modified, blunt horn that was a pommel, and looked down at Shi. "What you waiting for? Come on."

Reluctantly, Shi clambered up and settled behind me, then wrapped his arms around my chest.

"Remember," I told Tali. "Take it easy. Shi isn't used to this yet."

Shi screamed as Tali thundered across the clearing then launched. In seconds, we were miles from home and darting through the air like we were about to go supersonic.

Was good? she asked directly into my mind.

Very, I agreed, trying to conceal my mirth. *But I don't think Shi feels the same way about it.*

Why Shi scream?

He's adjusting to how powerful you are.

Tali is fastest dragon.

Are you sure you can morph so far with us both? It's risky.

No risk. Did before, remember?

Only a short distance.

Is scared?

It's 'are scared,' Tali.

Kifo are scared then?

I smiled. She had her own way of speaking, and always had. Guess there was no point trying to change her now. *A little. But I trust you, so let's do this.*

I turned as the air whipped my hair and told Shi, "Get ready. We're about to morph."

"What? No, wait!"

Pain engulfed me as Tali, and therefore her passengers, become nothing but pure energy. Ripped apart by the Necroverse and reassembled somewhere else. Never as all-encompassing as when I morphed alone, it nevertheless had the usual effects, so as I gasped, and let the pain disperse, the main thing on my mind was that I wished I'd brought sandwiches.

Tali had arrived directly outside Charles' weird Art Deco monstrosity of a house; I shuddered as I took in the wrongness of it. But with no time for architectural criticism, I slid from the saddle and landed beside a gasping Shi.

"Thank you, Tali. Please hide around the side of the house. Stay out of sight."

"Yeah, thanks for the ride. I think," grunted Shi, wiping sweat from his furrowed brow. He gathered his dark hair and squeezed it as if wringing it out, then whipped it to one side so he had easy access to his sword.

As Tali nodded, then crunched across the gravel, her body fading from sight and Necrosenses, I pulled out Ziggy and felt immediate comfort as I gripped the wooden shaft of the default club. Even after so many years, I couldn't believe I had such an utterly awesome magical weapon. The wizard I bought it off was a collector, not a warrior, and had been happy to part with it for the right price, even though owning anything made by the fae was extremely rare. I was sure there were still many things to discover about my weapon, but being able to change into any object I desired was good enough for me so far.

Without a word, Shi and I crept towards the house, then stopped either side of the open front door. I quickly tried to call Charles again but there was no answer, so after stowing my phone, and with a nod to Shi, he eased into the house and took the right side while I followed and pinned myself against the left wall.

There was no sign of anyone, but I could smell them. A sickly-sweet scent of timelessness. Shi sniffed deeply, then poked out his tongue to taste the air, the wolf part of him giving him a heightened sense of smell and hearing above my own impressive Necrosenses.

He eased over to me, closing the door silently as he came, then whispered, "I smell vampire."

I nodded. "How many?"

"Three. Maybe. It's hard to be precise. Two males, one female. What the fuck?"

"No idea, but they'll be listening to this. Their hearing is better than yours. Where are they?"

The air shifted and three blurry shapes darted from the open stairwell leading to the basement. "We're right here," hissed a handsome male as he bared his teeth.

"This will be fun," clapped the beautiful redhead, her many facial piercings glinting off the light pouring through the windows.

"It's an annoyance, nothing more," said the other man, dressed casually in jeans and dark t-shirt much like his companions. Although the other two were more punk looking, with rips in their jeans, heavy boots, and tattoos galore, whereas he was just a regular-looking guy, albeit with bloodied eyes and oversized canines.

"What do you want?" I asked, knowing more distance between us could improve our odds of getting out of here alive, but also knowing one sudden move would see them upon us.

"What business is it of yours?" sneered the most normal looking of the bunch.

"More to the point, what business do you have here, mate?" asked Shi, now back to looking relaxed and cocky.

"We come for the basement-dweller. The Archivist."

"Why? And how did you get in?"

"We have our ways," sneered tattoo guy.

"Vamp shit?" mused Shi.

"Enough!" the leader spat. "You will let us go below or we will destroy you both."

"Much as Arch is a pain in the ass, I'm not letting you in there with all those... Ah, I get it."

"I don't," shrugged Shi.

"They want Arch, but more importantly they want his books. They're nothing but dirty thieves."

"Our business is none of yours," said the leader. "You will give us access."

"I've had way too busy a morning for this crap," I sighed.

"I'm feeling fresh as a daisy," grinned Shi as he reached up and slowly pulled his sword from its scabbard.

"You will give us access," repeated Mr. Normal.

The three vampires smiled in anticipation as they closed in. The force of his words powered by his corrupted magic twisted and pounded into my skull, the air so weighted I almost sank to my knees under the pressure, but Shi and I were no novices at this game, and I especially had whispers of my own. Maybe not a match for their combined power, but I still had a trick or two up my sleeve.

As I feigned a stagger, I sent my instructions and will into Ziggy and thrust out with the club as it shifted into a ruby red spear aimed straight for the lead vampire's heart.

He dodged aside and laughed as he grabbed Ziggy and yanked.

Big mistake.

Armless Fun

Ziggy shifted into a barbed length of twisted steel. As the vampire yanked, so the razor-sharp metal tore through muscle and bone, severing half his fingers and cutting through his palm so deep that the rest of them merely hung on by wishful thinking.

His eyes turned black as he released Ziggy and hissed. His companions chuckled as their leader glared at them, then he too laughed as he lifted up his hand to inspect the damage. The deep incision knitted together, the fingers sprouted and grew rapidly, and in a moment the hand was as good as new.

"Didn't think we'd come visiting without feeding first, did you?" he sneered, nodding to his companions who spread out, following his wordless order.

Clearly, the fight was on.

"Tell me again why we're here protecting Arch?" said Shi.

"Good question. Because he asked nicely, I guess. And he said he might do something we'd all regret. Dunno, but there's no choice now."

I morphed, coming up behind the smaller vampire, and thrust Ziggy at the base of his spine. He whipped around and jumped back simultaneously, his vampire speed astonishing. The hair at the back of my neck shifted and I ducked just as a clawed hand shot out, easily powerful enough to crush my head or gouge out flesh.

Shi caught my attention as he danced past, sword swishing, the female vampire laughing. Her nose rings jangled as she rubbed a finger over them; for some reason, it seemed utterly perverse.

I morphed back to the kitchen to get a moment's grace. The two males were on me in a heartbeat, a blur of deadly menace as they reached for me, only Ziggy's cold steel stopping my guts being ripped out. With a shove, I stepped back, then sped around the expansive island and studied them for a moment, trying to get their measure.

Both smiled with pleasure, lost to the fight, the anticipation of blood clearly their motive now, Arch and his treasure forgotten. Already hyped on the blood of their victims, and oozing vitality and strength, they craved more and wouldn't be satisfied until they received what they desired.

We were undoubtedly a prize. Adept Necros with magical abilities, and also elven blood running through our veins. Sure, Shi might have only been a quarter elf, and me an eighth, but if Arch was to be believed, it would make our blood more potent than anything these clowns had ever known. The power they'd possess didn't bear thinking about. What I was surprised at was that they'd teamed up. Usually vamps lived alone their whole lives, unless they turned some unfortunate. Was that what this was? A master and two acolytes?

"Ah, that's it?" I said smugly. "We have the big boss man and two minions. You both new to this game, are you?"

"New?" growled tattoo guy. "I have been a vampire for over a century. And she has been part of our family for nigh on fifty years. Our maker blessed us, and we have been together ever since."

"Enough with this," snapped the leader. "We aren't here to chat with this human. You will give us access to the Archivist or die."

"And then you still won't be able to get in."

"Maybe not now, but we will eventually. I had hoped to save the energy needed to break through the door, but it can be done. It will be done."

"Then have at it. Be my guest. Say hi to Arch when you get in there. But trust me, he won't be in the best of moods."

"You joke at a time like this? Prepare to die."

They came at me from either side of the island. I hopped up and straddled the sink, then yanked the extendable tap, pushed the red button, and sprayed scalding hot water into the faces of first one, then the other.

As they screamed, and clutched their blistering skin, I swung Ziggy—now a sword—at the head of the leader. He sensed it and ducked, but Ziggy scalped his lustrous hair and the skin beneath clean off. It fell onto the counter, a bloody wig that I felt almost compelled to stomp on for fear it might scamper off.

With my whispers slamming down the other vampire, I hacked at his neck, the magic holding him in place just for a split-second, but it was enough. Ziggy lodged deep into his clavicle and I yanked to get him free, but he was stuck.

The vamp grabbed my arm and flung me from the island, but I kept a firm grip and as I spun aside so Ziggy was freed with a sudden spurt of blood. I rolled several times, then leapt to my feet, a wide stance for what I knew was inevitable.

Shi was battling the laughing woman who was dancing around him while she taunted my father with childish name-calling. Shi seemed rather amused by the whole thing.

And then he was gone.

I expected him to have morphed behind her, and she spun, clearly anticipating the same, but Shi didn't materialize.

Where was he?

He grinned at me from behind the lead vamp as his sword swung fast and accurate at the vampire's head. A moment too late, the vampire's attuned senses told him to duck, but the blade hacked through flesh and I relished watching his head fall from his shoulders.

It didn't. Just as Ziggy had, the steel sank deep into enhanced flesh and wouldn't budge even as Shi strained to release his weapon.

With a snarl, the startled vampire reached out and clamped down on Shi's hands. Shi grunted as pressure beyond the ability of a human was applied, and we both knew his fingers would be crushed in a moment.

With little choice, he morphed away, his sword still stuck in the vampire's neck.

The woman darted over to join her comrades as they turned, blisters healing on their smug faces. The scalped one's skin had partly healed and fresh hair sprouted from the still-bloodied scalp.

Knowing I'd be paying for this, I nevertheless morphed a mere foot, grabbed Shi's sword as it fell from the healing neck wound, then hopped back several steps to give myself breathing room.

They were on me in a second. I stumbled back then caught the corner of the table, grabbed a chair to stabilize, but it slipped from under me and I crashed to the hard tiles.

Three smiling vampires loomed over me, eyes black orbs of lust, teeth bared, lost to their own particular brand of insanity. Another morph so soon was out of the question. I'd get nowhere, and be a gibbering wreck afterwards, so there was only one thing I could do.

"Wait! I'll give you the code so you can get to Arch."

"Really?" The head vamp raised his eyebrows in suspicion. "Why?"

"Um, you know, because I'm a nice guy. Or, and you might have guessed this already, I don't want to be drained by a bunch of fucktwats."

"Did he just call us fucktwats?" asked the woman, chuckling. "I like it."

"The code," insisted the leader.

"Sorry, changed my mind," I laughed as Shi reappeared, grabbed his sword, then morphed once more and slashed without mercy at the back of all three necks the moment he could.

They hissed as they darted away then regrouped in front of me as Shi doubled over, the pain taking him, but it gave me the moment I needed to grab the chair and stand as Ziggy shifted into a wide trident. I grunted as I shoved forward with strength born of whispers.

Each prong pierced a vampire, but they looked down at their torsos and laughed as they gripped the trident and shunted it at me, forcing me back.

Shi hacked at their legs ineffectively as they easily glided aside, then we grouped close and confronted the vampires, seemingly having a jolly old time of it at our expense.

And then the basement door slammed shut as Arch stood there, looking sporty and athletic in his Kill Bill tracksuit, the yellow stripes stark against his dark hair and pale complexion. If he wasn't reading his books, he was watching old movies, and he loved Tarantino more than any other director. Guess the blood appealed.

Moving as athletically as he looked, Arch shot across the open plan interior like Mai attacking a dirty footprint, and snatched up the female vampire then proceeded to slam her headfirst into Charles' spotless white wall. With a sickly squelch, her head caved in and she was unceremoniously dropped.

Arch spun, eyes dark, fangs bared, as he squared off to the two remaining vampire intruders, Shi and I seemingly forgotten. With a shrug, I holstered Ziggy so I could shake out my hands and get the blood flowing, then cricked my neck, certain this fight was far from over for either me or Shi.

"I'm guessing this is Arch," said Shi, smirking.

"I can't believe you haven't met. How come? You've been around longer than me."

"Charles and his secrets. Although, I knew about this. But I haven't been here for a long time, and before that things weren't always very relaxed, if you get my drift. We had issues, is what I'm saying. Not his fault, but it is what it is."

"When you two have quite finished with your little chat, we have business to attend to," sighed Arch with a frown.

"Thought you were handling it now," I shrugged. "It's your mess, after all. They've come for your books."

"Not my books. One book in particular, I suspect," said Arch, casting a questioning glance at the leader.

"Where is it?" he hissed, baring his fangs as if that would intimidate Arch.

"Can't remember. I'm sure I put it somewhere."

"What book?" I asked.

"I recently acquired a rather interesting old tome about the elves. For Charles, you understand. It's invaluable, with priceless information. I'm guessing they want it."

"We do. And we will have it," said the leader as he crossed the distance between them in a flash and shunted Arch into the wall beside the fallen body of his comrade.

"The one you showed me?" I asked.

"No. Another. Much more focused on what you need."

"Let's not give away all our secrets," snapped Shi.

"Ah, the wolf-man," said Arch with a wicked smile. "We meet at last. The prodigal son."

"Again, let's not tell them everything. This isn't Vampires Reunited."

"We know of your family. We know of all of you. And we want that book."

"Why?" I asked.

"As you said, best not to give away the secrets," the leader sighed, then punched out so fast I figured Arch would be mush. Seemingly, he was prepared, and dodged expertly as the fist cracked the wall and plaster fell as dust while Arch dashed around the vampires, grabbed me and Shi, and raced for the front door.

As he opened it, the vamps were right behind us. I yanked Shi aside as Arch sidestepped the other way as they both punched out hard enough to penetrate our skulls.

Then all was still as Tali in her human form, regal and deadly looking, stepped delicately into the room on her pretty, bare feet.

"Who is friends?" she asked me.

"Well, me and Shi, obviously. And, er, the one in the striped tracksuit. The other two are definitely enemies."

"What is this?" asked the lead vampire. "You dare bring a... a what? Witch?" He studied Tali, then his eyes widened and he exclaimed, "A dragon?"

"What are you talking about?" asked the younger vampire, turning to him then back to Tali. "She's hot, I'll give her that, but she isn't a dragon."

"Silence! Look closely. Look at her eyes. Priceless. My, what a surprise." He licked his lips; two pinpoints of heat sprang up on his cheeks.

"Must kill bad men," said Tali. "Mustn't know Tali is here."

"Why did you come?" I asked. "You were meant to remain hidden."

"Tali will help. Is good practice. Charles and Kifo said must be woman more times. Speak to people. Am talking now."

"Yes, but to two vampires. And there's a dead one over there." I pointed to the fallen woman, then gasped as she stirred. Her caved-in head had already returned to its regular form, and although covered in dark bruises, she was shaking her head and clambering cautiously to her feet.

"We aren't that easy to kill," admitted Arch. "I thought she'd sustained too much damage, but clearly not."

"Tali will snap."

Before even the vampires had a chance to move, Tali had morphed to the damaged woman, twisted her head around a full one-eighty and was now back at our side.

"Bloody hell," blurted Shi.

"We can handle this," I told Tali again. "But while you're here, I guess..."

"We will leave," said the rigid vampire in charge. "Apologies for any inconvenience. We do not wish to offend one as glorious as you. If I may?" He reached out with shaking fingers and gently took Tali's hand, then raised it to his lips and kissed it delicately. Tali giggled, then frowned at the noise emanating from her ripe lips.

"Why man kiss hand?"

"It's a sign of respect and admiration," I explained.

"Is nice. Kifo will kiss Tali?"

"Maybe another time," I spluttered, events taking a very unexpected turn.

Tali nodded, then snatched out, grabbed the vampires hand, and twisted until his arm cracked as the bone broke. Smiling at me, she yanked so hard the entire appendage snapped away.

She studied the arm, frowning, then slammed it into the head of the other stunned vampire. He flew right across the room and Tali was upon him before he landed. She growled and shrieked as she battered him repeatedly, then, seemingly finding the arm an ineffective weapon, flung it against a window and clawed out his eyes with her slender fingers.

The vampire screamed wildly so Tali punched out his teeth then bent, calm and ladylike, gripped his head, and with a grunt, heaved back and up as she stood. Neck bones snapped as flesh stretched then split, until the head was attached by nothing but sinew. It came away with a squelch. Tali studied it as you would an interesting piece of driftwood washed up on the shore then threw it aside carelessly.

With the armless vampire understandably distracted, I ran through his throat with Ziggy, then stabbed at his heart and cut his carotid artery for good measure before wiping the blade clean even though it wasn't strictly necessary—Ziggy remained clean no matter what I did. Gore seemed to just slither off him like he was negatively charged.

"Is that enough?" I asked Arch.

"I would assume so. That much damage should be impossible to come back from." Arch kicked the corpse just to be sure, then smiled. "Wonderful! That wasn't as bad as I'd expected. Well done, all of you."

"Gee, thanks. Anything else we can do for you?"

Arch suddenly seemed to collapse in on himself as he stared past Shi and out of the front door. His already pale face turned ashen before he spun and bolted for the basement. The door banged open and he raced down the stairs, the dull reverberation of the other door slamming against the wall a clear sign he'd entered his lair once more.

"Guess we better go check on him," I said.

"Tali will wait outside. Not like house. Is wrong."

"Thanks for the help," I called after her, but she was already gone.

"That was..." stammered Shi.

"Intense?"

"Yeah," he chuckled, "intense. She's incredible. Did you see what she did?" I stared at him. "Course you did. Mate, she's awesome. My grandchildren will be absolutely kick-ass."

"Don't go getting any ideas," I warned, rushing after the man I still couldn't quite think of as my father, especially when he called me "mate" the same as everyone else, including his own father.

"I'm just saying that was impressive. Gross, but impressive."

We turned to survey the brutal aftermath of a dragon on the defensive. "She's certainly still ferocious as a woman. Charles will be pissed. He hates a mess."

"Then he should have answered his phone and sorted this out himself. Where is he? I thought he was coming over today to finalize things and check the job went okay?"

"He was, but it's still early. He was arriving after lunch. Guess he got sidetracked or something happened. You don't think the elves have him again, do you?"

"Nope. He's got what he wanted, so the one thing we can be certain of is he won't let them get their prissy hands on him again. Not until we go to annoy them, anyway." With a grin, Shi turned back to the stairwell and whistled as he descended like he'd been down there a hundred times before.

No Skin in the Game

I let the door click closed behind me, then stood beside a shocked Shi and called, "What was that about, Arch? Can't you handle your own business? We aren't your bloody bodyguards. And you got Tali involved."

"I did nothing of the sort. You should keep a tighter rein on your pet."

I stormed across the priceless Persian rugs and got right up in his face, uncaring even as his eyes turned red. "You ever, and I mean ever, say something derogatory about her again and I will make it my life's mission to destroy you. Understand?"

"Apologies. I was merely being flippant."

"Watch your words," I warned. "She's not a pet. Tali's bonded to me, and me to her. We are the same. We are free to make our own way, but choose to be together. You insult her, you insult me. She's not a pet," I barked, so close to attacking him I had a hard time controlling the bloodlust as it surged through my icy veins.

"Easy there, fellas," said Shi, sauntering over, shaking his head at me. "Cool it. And Arch, you got something to say?"

"I already apologized, but yes, I am truly sorry. It was in bad taste and she saved the day. What a wonderful, er, woman? Dragon? I've been longing to meet her for so many years. Now I have. And as a woman. So incredible. I heard of her progress, but never knew she was so stunningly attractive. You are one lucky man," he said, smiling lewdly.

"It isn't like that."

"No? But for how long? As you said, you are bonded. That is as close as a vampire and his chosen one. Bonded by blood for eternity, never able to remain apart for the pain it causes. There is no closer connection."

"You ever turned anyone to be your, what do you call it? Acolyte?"

"Not an acolyte, more a life-partner. But no, never. I prefer to be alone, make my own decisions, and answer to nobody. Besides, all that trouble is such a chore. Them having to be interred for a hundred years in limbo, waiting for the right time, then having to return and deliver the final bite? It's so tiresome. Who has the time for such things?" He waved it away as if it were nothing, not worthy of his consideration.

"Anyone going to introduce us?" asked Shi, perusing the shelves.

"Shi, this is Arch. Arch, this is Shi," I grunted, my mood sour.

After they said their hellos, neither seemingly particularly interested in the other, I asked the burning question.

"What was the book those other vampires wanted?"

"Ah," said Arch, beaming, "a rare tome indeed. I showed you my other book on the elves written by the Scottish witch, Blair, who had visited the realm, did I not?"

"You did. It gave some insight, but you only discussed it briefly."

"Well, this is even more interesting. Written by an outcast, a true elf, and much more recent, it has fascinating information about the whole race."

"I won't ask where you got it."

"Good idea," he grinned, sliding onto his leather wingback with a sigh, then taking up a thick book from the ornate side table to this right. "It's bound in human skin. How degenerate they are," he laughed.

Shi and I took a seat on the Chesterfield, the polished leather as shiny as Tali's wings, and we both groaned. I could have closed my eyes and nodded off. Early mornings were never my forte, and this hadn't been so much an early start as hardly worth going to bed.

"What have you learned? Why did Charles want it?" asked Shi.

"Our lord and master has been very keen for me to gather any and all information pertaining to the elves. With your adventure looming, it's a sensible approach, but information is scant, verging on non-existent. I believe I now have the only two books with anything approaching reliable information."

"Nice," I said dreamily. "That's wonderful."

Shi laughed, bringing me out of my half-sleep. I glared at him, then sat more upright and forced myself to stay awake.

"Indeed. In case Charles and I don't get a chance to discuss this further, although we have already spoken at length, here are the, ahem, highlights."

Shi and I both leaned forward, keen to learn whatever we could before we left. So far, we knew basically nothing whatsoever about the elven homeworld, and had zero idea how to even find Lake Elinor. With a million and one questions we'd like answered, this might at least give us an idea of what we were up against.

"Any maps?" I asked. "Maps would be awesome."

"Yes, lots of maps. And one you will be very keen to inspect. But be careful. This book is priceless."

"Can I take some pictures?" I asked. "We'll need them for our trip."

"Useless, I'm afraid, which is something I learned from this text. Our technology will not work there. None of it. No digital watches, phones, nothing."

"What about our Necro abilities?" asked Shi. "And weapons like Ziggy?"

"All fine. It may not be earth, but it is part of the Necroverse. A much more magical place than our homeworld. Abilities, skills, etc. will work just fine. But, of course, that comes with one very large problem. Humans cannot function there if unaccompanied by a dragon. They need the strength, the immortality, the sheer presence of such a creature to survive. The only other way, and this is what is most interesting, is if you can find an elf willing to assist you. Clearly, they are from their own world, so if you can get a friendly elf to remain by your side, you will be able to be yourselves."

"And what are the chances of that happening?" I wondered.

"I'd say about zero. Elves are not friendly to our kind. Any of us. They see us as little but dirt beneath their feet. Yes, they follow the exploits of some Necros, reveling in the misery many of our kind face because of the yearly Necronotes, but even they don't know the source of such notes, although they are spared the ignominy of such a disturbing yearly birthday treat."

"How do they watch us?" asked Shi.

"Cameras inside miniature portals. They also seemingly have access to the Necrodrones somehow, and often important battles are televised in huge arenas especially for such sport. It's all rather disturbing, and an insight into their mindset," he said happily. "They like to watch us murder one another, have no sympathy, no empathy, and certainly no desire to assist us. You have rogue elements like Eleron who enjoy coming and stirring up trouble, but most elves would see it as utterly beneath them to even breathe our air, let alone interact with a human."

"They really are something," chuckled Shi.

"Indeed. And not to be underestimated. Shi, they are so different to humans that it's hard to understand how truly alien a species they are. Pride comes before all else. Their entire culture seems to be based on it. Reputation and saving face are at the cornerstones of their existence. Ceremony and tradition are so intrinsic to their life that it's part of their being. Think how Great Britain used to be, how important royalty, our traditions, our hierarchy of class were, and still are to a degree. Times that by a hundred, a thousand, and you have the elves."

"So, a bunch of pompous twats then," I said.

"You could say that. Or you could say they are very respectful of their traditions and believe how they do things is the right way. But it goes deeper than that. Much deeper. They remember so much, they need something to keep the continuity going. Their lives are so extended, many thousands of years in some cases, that they have systems in place to ensure that as a whole their race is rather peaceful. Sure, you get factions and in-fighting, plays for power, and feuds can last millennia, but they stand by their rules, their way of doing things, and they do not like change."

"Who does?" grunted Shi.

"Not us three, but we are not the norm, as the dead vampires upstairs are testament to. Which, by the way, Charles will be very annoyed about."

"Don't blame us," I said. "You're the one who called needing help. And it's because Charles wanted this bloody book. I'm sure you can call in some cleaners to sort it out."

"And have strangers in the house? But yes, there are ways and means of rectifying the problem. Maybe I'll venture outside, dispose of the mess personally."

"That's the spirit," I said, smiling. "It'll do you good to get out. Nothing like burying bits of vampire to get you out of your funk."

"It is not a funk," snapped Arch, face darkening. "It's a loathsome medical condition I have spent a lifetime trying to conquer. You shouldn't make fun of someone's issues like that."

"Sorry, you're right. So, what else have you discovered from your new book?"

"That you're going to have a tough time surviving." Arch closed his prize and placed it carefully on the side table before meeting our eyes solemnly. "They do not take kindly to any form of disruption, yet are very complacent about certain things because of their nature. They are beyond self-assured, and utterly confident in their abilities. They will not expect lowly humans to even consider invading their homeworld. It's unprecedented and beyond foolhardy, so they won't envision anyone attempting such a thing. But the moment you're discovered, you'll be fighting a losing battle. And mark my words, it is one you will lose. A few of you against an entire race of superior beings is not a fight you can ever dream of winning."

"Way to put a downer on things," grumbled Shi.

"I'm just being pragmatic and honest. My best advice? Do what you have to do and get out of there. Fast. Speed is of the essence. Don't dawdle, don't admire the scenery, and certainly don't let any of them see you. It's an archaic society, and even though they have technology, it's limited. Mostly, they live closely with nature. But don't let that fool you. They aren't fearful, they aren't kind, and they aren't going to like you. Be fast, be silent, and be on your guard constantly. Good luck to you."

"Wow, thanks. We appreciate that, don't we, Shi?"

"We do. But what's your interest in all this?" Shi cast a suspicious glance at Arch before looking at me like I knew the answer.

"Oh, ha, yes, this certainly isn't as altruistic as it might seem. Very astute. I want you to succeed because I want Charles to remain alive. It's as simple as that. I love my home, I adore my sanctuary, and I prefer not having to concern myself with the mundane trivialities of survival. I can't imagine having to find somewhere else to live, or having somebody else residing upstairs. Charles deals with everything running a household entails, and I like it that way. I hardly ever see him. He leaves me to my work, and yet I know he is there when needed."

"Apart from today," I reminded him. "Where the hell is he?"

"Off on spook business," said Shi, seemingly no longer concerned.

"So, yes, I have my reasons for wanting you all to make a success of this. Plus, and I'm as surprised as you, I like you, Kifo. And even you, Shi. You are Charles' son, his family, so I wish you the best." Arch sighed, then closed his eyes, and his body began to shake as if her were fighting inner demons. Abruptly, he rose, snatched up the book, and reached out with it to me. "Here, take it. Quickly, before I reconsider."

"Are you sure?" I asked, rising, then taking the book from his shaking hands.

"No, that's why I'm trembling. Hurry."

I tugged, and reluctantly he released the book then turned and sank back into his chair.

"It feels warm," I noted, running my hand over the leather. "Human skin," I whispered. "I forgot."

"Yes, and let that be a reminder to you both. They will think nothing of using your skin as a prize. And bring the book back to me. It's beyond valuable, and it would be a shame to lose it."

"You can count on us," said Shi as he stood and nodded.

"Good. Now leave, before I change my mind about the book. Tell Charles to get in touch. We have a few things to discuss." With a wave, we were dismissed.

Neither of us could get out of there fast enough. Arch was a hard person to deal with, and I was never relaxed in his company. He was like a caged animal, and I always got the feeling he could turn feral at any moment. The basement really was the best place for him. It was just a shame he didn't stay there for good.

The true extent of the carnage became apparent once we returned upstairs. Charles would throw a fit. Then again, maybe not. He wasn't some paper-pusher who never got his hands dirty. He was a true Necro, and death and the foulness that came with it was unavoidable for our kind.

"What now?" asked Shi.

"I guess we go home. I don't like leaving the place in this condition, but Arch and Charles will have to deal with it."

"Wherever Charles is."

"Think it's worth checking Eloise's? Maybe he's there." Shi grunted, but said nothing. "What?"

"I haven't seen her in a long time, and I don't plan on visiting any time soon either."

"What's the problem? She's your great-aunt, isn't she?"

"The problem? You have to ask? You met her, so you know what she's like. I can't stand all that upper-class bullshit. It makes me want to burn the bloody house down."

"I know what you mean. It's a bit much, and she's pretty intense. But you really haven't seen her for years?"

"I try to avoid her. We don't get on. Look, you know the story now. I haven't been around much for a very long time. I kept a low profile even before you were born, and once you were, I did my best to give you a decent childhood. I kept you away from Eloise and her nonsense, and Charles and I had our issues too, but we were kinda close in our own way. But after... After I did what I did, killed your mother, my wife, a woman I adored, I became a different man. A vagrant, a traveler, always roaming. And I kept out of your life because I thought it was for the best, so that meant staying away from Charles. Sure, I checked in, got regular updates about you, but I wasn't involved. I couldn't be."

"I understand. You did what you thought was best."

"But it wasn't, was it? I abandoned you. I know I did. And now you're all grown up, a man. I missed out on so much, but I couldn't risk hurting you. Or Charles. Or putting either of you in the position where it could be you or me. And now look what's happened. To get this damn brooch it almost happened all over again. I could have killed either of you. The thing inside me took over and I attacked you. If you hadn't clobbered me, I would have torn you both apart."

"But you didn't."

"No, but it almost happened. I can't even begin to explain how stressed out I was, still am, and I can't stand the thought of going through it again. I will not kill more of my family. But I can't do this without you. Understand? I'm in a terrible, gut-wrenching quandary and I feel like an utter fucking lowlife for asking this of you."

"We're family. You're my father, and I'll do anything to help you. I truly understand why you did what you did. You don't need to apologize over and over for it. I get it. We're together now, that's what counts, and the past is just that. The past. So let's kick elven ass and get you healed, okay?"

Shi smiled as he slapped me on the back then said, "Aw, come here," and grabbed me in a bear hug. He smelled of the forest. He smelled like my father.

I wrapped my arms around him and said, "We'll get through this. I know it's a lot for you to handle, and I know how risky it is, but we'll do this. Okay?"

We broke apart and he nodded. "Thank you."

"Father and son. Now all we need is grandad," I chuckled.

"Did someone mention me?" asked Charles as he clicked the door closed and stood, face turning from a smile to ashen, as he took in the state of his home.

Broken Home

Charles raised an eyebrow as we stood there like naughty schoolboys, not the assassins we were.

"Um, we can explain," offered Shi.

"Indeed."

"Arch called. He had a spot of bother. It got messy," I admitted.

"Indeed."

"And there might be a few heads dotted about the place. And a dash of blood on the wall. Maybe a few smears on the windows. And you might want to give your tap a nice clean. Maybe a spray with something."

"I'd just raze it to the ground and start again," said Shi.

"Not helping," I told him.

"This place always felt a bit off anyway," continued Shi. "The architecture is all wrong. It's like a mausoleum, not a home."

"It's how I liked it. Simple. Clean lines. And no vampire bits making the place looking untidy," said Charles, shaking his head as he stared at us.

"Blame Arch," I shrugged.

"Actually, you've only got yourself to blame," said Shi.

"How so?" asked Charles, a wry smile spreading across his fine features.

"That's right," I said, warming to the idea now. "Arch called us because he couldn't get hold of you. If you'd answered his call, you could have been the one spreading vampire juice up the walls."

"I would have been much more discreet. You can believe that."

"And how exactly would you have dealt with them?" I asked, intrigued.

"By giving them the book so they'd leave, then going to their home and making their taps dirty. By letting their blood spill on their own property, rather than mine. My, what a horror show you two have created."

"Actually, Tali might have helped a little. Hence the heads ripped from shoulders thing," I admitted. "And the arm."

"We need to up our training with her," noted Charles. "She's supposed to be acting more human, not more dragon."

"She tore that guy's head off in a very ladylike manner," laughed Shi.

"Almost elegant," I agreed with a chuckle.

"Your sense of humor is most unseemly." Charles frowned as he marched over to the island and gasped as he inspected the tap.

Our spirits higher than they maybe should have been, we nevertheless joined him, three grown-up men staring at a ridiculously expensive tap like it held answers to an important question.

"Let this be a lesson to you both," said Charles, noting the blood spatters across his cupboard doors and the bits of vampire brain lodged in the plughole.

"What's the lesson?" I asked.

"Don't buy overpriced taps. I always hated the damn thing anyway." Charles shrugged, then turned and smiled. "I'll get the cleaners in. I have an arrangement. Now, shall we get down to business?"

"Whoa, wait just one minute," I said. "Where were you? All this over a book and you weren't available? What gives?"

"If you must know, I was making arrangements."

"What arrangements?" asked Shi.

"In case I, in case we, don't return."

"Oh. Way to put a downer on the day," said Shi.

"Seriously?" I asked Shi. "I was up in the middle of the bloody night dealing with insane Necros about to murder innocent young girls, then chasing vampires and dealing with Arch, and you call Charles buggering off a downer? Oh, I forgot, you were having a nice lie-in while I dealt with the crazies."

"Hey, that was your job, and I knew you didn't want me interfering. And besides, you wouldn't have let me come."

"True." I asked Charles, "What arrangements did you make?"

"Just ensuring nothing happens to our property, our wards."

"Our wards? You mean the safeguards to our homes?"

"No, I mean your wards actually. Those under your care. Have you thought about what would happen if you didn't return one day? If you were killed?"

"I try not to," I mumbled.

"As do I. But none of us are infallible. These things need arranging. What would become of Nava, or Mai, or Tali, if you were no longer around?"

"See, this is why I want a simple life. Being an assassin isn't conducive to long-term relationships or complications."

"You sure it isn't just because you enjoy being alone and eating cereal nude at nine at night?" laughed Shi.

"Who told you?" I blurted. "Um, not that I've ever done that."

"I would."

"When you've both quite finished." Charles shook his head, bemused by our high spirits despite the grim situation. "Someone needs to consider these things. And more importantly, someone needs to actually act on such thoughts. I am always prepared, always, but there were a few loose ends that needed tidying up, and I apologize for being unavailable. Now, would you care to know what I have decided?"

"How come you get to decide what happens to anyone? You may be my blood, and my boss, but you don't get to run my life," I said, suddenly less jolly.

"Same here," said Shi, voice gruff. "Not that I have anything to leave anyone, or anyone to leave it to if we all croak it," he admitted. "But the principle still stands."

"Assassins need to think about these things. I know it's rather uncommon for ones like us to bother with such matters, but I prefer to be thorough."

"Says the posh jerk who doesn't tie his shoelaces without getting an application form signed in triplicate," said Shi.

"I'll have you know, I'm rather a maverick in our line of work," said Charles sourly.

"Fine, what did you do? What did you decide for me?" I asked.

"Your property is your own matter, and a mere trifle," said Charles, waving the matter away. "But for Nava and Mai I have asked a friend to go and look after them should anything happen to you. One of the witches who helped put the wards protecting your home in place."

"Have I met her?"

"No, but she is a kindly soul and will take good care of things. She will also assist Tali in any way she can, should it come to that. I wanted this done, and it should have been discussed, but I left it rather late. I apologize."

"Damn, now you're making me feel bad. Why haven't I dealt with this?"

"We don't. We put things off, we procrastinate, and we believe we are invincible. But there comes a time when such matters must be handled. Now they are. Sorry for intruding on your personal affairs, but at least I know things will be taken care of properly. And, more importantly, my dear aunt won't just take everything."

"She still could if she wanted to," said Shi, sounding bitter.

"She will not. We have, er, had words, and the matter is settled."

Shi and I exchanged a glance, but knew better than to press Charles when he clearly wasn't comfortable.

"I trust you on this, Charles. And I feel lame for not having arranged things myself. I should know better."

"Don't be too hard on yourself, my dear boy. I have had a very long time to put my own affairs in order, but it is only now that I have done so. We are facing almost insurmountable odds and traveling into the unknown, and this has thankfully awakened my own need to settle some personal affairs. Now it is done, and we can focus on what lies ahead."

"Which is?"

"Showing the elves that the human race isn't as much of a pushover as they believe."

"Although," said Shi, "we aren't actually fully human, are we? You're half-elf, so none of us are a hundred percent homo sapien."

"No, and that makes them think even less of us. But let's hope we can merely accomplish our task and not deal with any of them. That's the ideal best-case scenario, but you know what they say about the best laid plans of mice and men."

"It all goes to shit," grumbled Shi.

"Exactly," said Charles. "Now, I do believe we need to take our dear dragon and teach her at least a little about interacting in her human form. We have been lax in such matters, and time is now very pressing. Shall we?"

"Don't we even get a coffee first?" I asked. Charles cleared his throat as he nodded to the state of his kitchen. "Yeah, maybe you're right."

Tali was resting in full stealth-mode at the side of the house, but shifted easily into her human form. You'd have no idea she was capable of such barbarism by looking at her, let alone that she would happily inflict much worse damage.

"Do you think you would like to try walking through the city?" I asked.

"Tali can walk easily," she pouted. "Is simple."

"Yes, but this is different. There are other people around, and horses and carts. All kinds of things. You've only ever seen London from the air, or rooftops, not just wandered around and had to deal with things."

"Like in air."

"Of course. But remember what we said? That you need to learn how to interact with others? Go into a shop, talk to strangers, that kind of thing. We can do it now if you'd like."

"Will help?"

"Yes. And you've got much better at remaining in human form. You can do it for hours now, rather than minutes. This is all part of the training. You want to be a human woman sometimes, don't you?" I asked in a whisper, while the others pretended not to listen.

"So can be with Kifo. Not walk in dirty streets."

"I understand, but we go to the elven homeworld tomorrow, so we should get as much practice in as we possibly can. It will boost your confidence. Show you what you're capable of."

"Already confident. Can do anything," she shrugged.

"True. The last thing you need is more confidence. But you do need the practice. We've left it too late for you to learn much more, but every little helps. And while we're here, why not?"

"Will do for Kifo."

"That's great, my dear," said Charles, beaming.

"Then let's get this show on the road," said Shi, grinning at us.

"What's so amusing?" I asked.

"Just that you all seem oblivious to how awful an idea this is. Tali is a dragon, not a human, and this can go wrong in so many spectacular ways I wouldn't even know where to begin. But it's your decision."

"We're doing this for you! So Tali can be with us tomorrow. And not show her true nature."

"I know, and I appreciate it. But still, this is risky."

"Tali will be magnificent, same as she is in everything she does," said Charles.

"Let's just get this over with," I sighed, knowing Shi was right.

We exited the property and walked cautiously down the street, mindful of Tali's utter inexperience with such simple activities. She seemed to find the experience fascinating, marveling at the houses, the way the pavement felt on her bare feet, even stopping to inspect drains and ask questions about how sewage systems worked.

Us three men were sweltering under the intense afternoon heat, but Tali, her dragon nature coming to the fore, relished the feel of the sun on her body. I worried that she would burn as her skin was so pale, but reminded myself that this may be her human form and very real and solid, but it didn't work that way and she was still immortal with the skin of a dragon.

Ten minutes later, Shi told us he had several errands to run so left after we agreed to meet up later. My tension eased a little once he'd gone, as I worried less about something going wrong if it was just me and Charles looking out for Tali. Too many people offering their opinions on how she should act merely confused her, and made everything harder for her to understand.

We headed into a small commercial district, Charles in the lead, Tali and I staying close together. Although beyond strange for her, I was discovering I was finding the experience very odd, too. I became lost in her every move, mindful of how difficult and alien an environment this was, but also discovering how much I was enjoying being in her presence somewhere I'd never imagined possible.

It was easy to believe we were a couple just out shopping before heading home to cook an evening meal, maybe settle down afterward on the sofa with a glass of wine. Her every turn of the head, every footstep, every giggle of delight, or frown of distaste, was mesmerizing. I was absorbed by the sight, sound, and smell of her, not the city. She became my world, and I knew she felt the same way as much as the environment held her transfixed.

"How are you coping?" I asked as Charles moved a little further ahead.

"Like but not like. Want to run, then fly, and want to kill rude people. Why nobody look in eye?"

"It's always the same in big cities. People are more wary, more guarded, than in small towns or villages. Everyone keeps their head down and just gets on with their own business. And remember the riots I told you about?" Tali nodded. "That made everyone even more scared. And now we have the drones and cameras, and everyone is suspicious of authority. There's a nervousness, and rightly so. But yes, it isn't a very friendly place anymore, not that it ever was."

"Can go soon? Where is quiet?"

"Soon, but there are a few more things we need to do. I won't insist you must, but it is good for you. If you can handle London, you can handle anything. That's a true test of character."

"Prefer woods. Like home. Nice and quiet. Not people. So mean. Why woman shout?" Tali stopped and stared at a lone mother chastising a small boy. He was crying, face red, tiny hands bunched into fists as he stamped his foot, defiant despite the upset.

"I guess the boy has been naughty or isn't doing as he's told, so she's telling him off and reminding him how to behave. It's how children learn what's right and wrong and what's acceptable behavior."

"Child not just know what can do? Why told? Everyone know what want to do."

"Life doesn't work like that. You can't just do what you want to."

"Tali does."

"But that's different. And even you follow rules. You don't always just do what you feel like. Sometimes you do things to help me that you don't enjoy."

"Like walking in smelly street and not killing rude people?"

"Exactly. All creatures nurture their young and teach them how to behave, what to do. How to hunt, how to communicate, how to be independent."

"Kifo teach Tali those things," she said knowingly.

"Yes, some of them. Charles too. And you learned things from Nava, like how to share your food. And Mai taught you an incredible amount, like the importance of keeping things clean and tidy. There's plenty that is innate, but a lot that you only learn by example. So the boy is being told off by his mother and then he will have learned a valuable lesson. Parents have to repeat these lessons many thousands of times to do their very best to ensure the survival of their children. If they didn't get taught how to cross a road safely, they could get killed by a horse or cart.

It used to be worse when there were speeding vehicles, but it's still dangerous now. And children don't know they can get burned by fire, and so many other things like that I wouldn't know where to begin."

"Kifo did these things for Tali?" she asked, gazing into my eyes.

"I did. And it never stops. But now it's different because you are older and much wiser, but you being a human is like starting all over again. You know what is safe when you are a dragon, how to behave, but that's nowhere near as scary as trying to make your way in the world as a human being. It's a terrifying world we live in, and it does its best to break us, so we need someone to look out for us. To love us."

"Tali loves Kifo."

"And I love you too. Come on, we shouldn't stare. It's rude, and people don't like it."

"Why?"

"Because some things are private. A mother doesn't want other people gawping while she chastises her child."

"Why?"

"Fear of being judged. Humans worry what other people think of them. Even strangers."

"Is silly."

"Very. But that's how we're wired. I'm past crap like that, but even so, it's rude to stare. It's why everyone's so on edge. It's because they know they have absolutely no privacy when outside their homes. Every movement is tracked, monitored, and it makes people uneasy. This is why the streets are emptier than they have been in hundreds and hundreds of years. It's not difficult to imagine the government has done it on purpose as a way of controlling us. Keep the populace fearful and locked in their homes without actually forcing them."

"Humans are very strange."

"Like I said, you've still got a lot to learn, but you got that right. We are. Come on, Charles is waiting. It's time for your big test."

"Tali has exam?" she asked, looking slightly panicked.

"You could say that," I said, grinning.

Breaking Bread

"Just remember what we discussed," I told Tali, glancing nervously to Charles.

"You'll be fine, won't you, my dear?" Charles nodded to me, and beamed at Tali as he ran confident fingers through his short blond hair. His eyes, one green, one blue, sparkled with hardly concealed mirth.

"This isn't funny," I snapped. "Tali could shift back into dragon form inside and what then? This is a terrible idea."

"Tali can do. Am mighty dragon. Do anything. Easy to be woman. Can go in shop. Buy things."

"Do you remember what you do?" I asked.

"Pick loaf of bread. Sniff. Put on little table by pathetic man. Say want to buy. Give me now."

"It's a counter. That's what you call it," I explained again, shaking my head at Charles. She wasn't ready for this.

"Counter. Table that is not table is counter. Will buy bread," she insisted.

We stood beside the window, watching people coming and going from the small shop in a suburb where nobody knew me or Charles. For days we'd been trying to teach Tali how to act like a human being, but this was not her nature and she found the whole thing perplexing to say the least. Charles, and particularly me, found it nothing but frustrating.

I feared not only for Tali's health and mental wellbeing—as who knew what kind of stress this put on her mind?—but for the consequences if this went wrong. They could be dire. Having a dragon suddenly materialize in a small room would most likely result in the death of innocents and put a halt to the whole sorry charade. Not to mention the utter chaos that would ensue.

"Remember, above all else, nobody must know of your existence. You are too rare and precious for others to discover you are a dragon. If this is too much, just say so now."

"He's right," said Charles, mirth waning. "Maybe we should go home. You have remained a secret for so many years. We must keep it that way. Other Necros would do anything to own you."

"Nobody own Tali," she hissed, her form wavering, giving a split-second glimpse of the violent dragon beneath.

Charles and I exchanged a look. This was not a good idea.

"No, of course not, my dear. I meant, others might come and try to take you. Coerce you. Gosh, I do believe I am getting flummoxed."

"That's a first," I chuckled, amused by his discomfort when he'd always been irritatingly unflappable.

"Indeed."

"Tali go. Buy bread from shop man."

Before we could stop her, Tali turned and strode towards the door.

With a shrug, Charles and I followed, watching what she did like two mad scientists observing their latest experiment.

The first obstacle was the door. We'd been through it many times, but Tali halted and stared at it, trying to get her dragon mind around the concept of using hands and figuring out how it functioned.

"This is our first mistake," noted Charles. "We've practiced with your front door, but not others."

"Is different," said Tali with a frown. Nevertheless, she reached out with pale, delicate-yet-strong fingers and pushed on the metal frame around the glass. She giggled as the door clicked open. "What sound just make?" she asked, touching her lips.

"You giggled. Like a laugh. I guess it's an instinct."

"Tali like. Buy bread now?" Without waiting for an answer, she glided into the shop on her bare feet.

We'd tried and tried to get her to wear something on her feet, or just create the image of wearing sandals or anything else, but after trying on real slippers and the resulting tirade of complaints and her coming close to an utter meltdown, there was no convincing her. Over the ensuing days, she'd suffered cuts and blisters walking barefoot, but now her feet were seemingly as tough as her dragon hide. She healed so rapidly anyway that no sooner was any damage caused to her human body than it was as good as new.

"What do now?" asked Tali as she stood in the middle of the small space, her arms limp by her side.

"Go and look at the loaves and pick one, then take it to the counter. Remember?"

"Yes. Tali know." She shuffled forward, stopped at the rows of bread neatly arranged in wicker baskets, and stared down at them. Then she bent, and sniffed several seedy loaves before grunting and turning to a stack of loaves the small sign said contained various herbs.

Tentatively, then seemingly finding an inner confidence in her ability to cope with this, she reached out and snatched up a loaf. "Smells good. Like how has green bits. Remind of home."

"It's got rosemary in it. I grow it in the herb garden," I told her.

With the loaf raised to her cute nose, Tali snorted deeply, then made a weird choking sound at the back of her throat.

Charles' eyes widened but he remained silent, watching her intently. We got a frown from a woman the opposite side of the racks, but then she went to make her purchase, leaving us alone.

"Is nice. Will buy." Tali then ripped off a huge chunk with her teeth and chewed loudly before blurting, "Taste good! Tali want more!" She waved the loaf around like it was a prize she wanted to show off.

Not knowing what to do or say, and Charles as flummoxed as I was, we hurried after her as she marched decisively over to the baker and slammed the loaf down on the counter.

"Is counter," she told him, rapping the wood with her knuckles.

"Um, sure is, pretty lady," he replied, staring at her. "Anything else I can get for you?"

"Have cheese?"

"Um, no, this is a bakery. We don't sell cheese."

"Man ask if Tali want anything else. Want cheese."

"That's not how shops work. You new to these parts, eh?"

"Tali live far away. Not go in shop before. Will buy bread."

"Okay," he said, confused. "You feeling a bit peckish, eh?" he asked, retrieving the bread and noting the chunk missing.

"Is Tali's," she growled, snatching the loaf back and hugging it tight to her chest.

"I was just checking it over for you. But sure, you keep hold of it."

"Tali buy bread."

"Yes, right."

Charles stepped forward and paid the baker while Tali clutched the loaf, then we all turned to leave. As we did, a harried-looking man in his thirties burst through the door and shouted out, "Got any poppy-seed loaves left?" to the baker.

"Over there," he said, pointing.

The man brushed past Charles, grunted as he caught him on the shoulder, then jumped into Tali's path and stopped dead in his tracks when she put a hand to his chest.

"Man will apologize. Nasty thing. Shoved Tali's friend. Is bad... What word?"

"Manners," I told her.

"What are you talking about, lady? Where you from?" he sneered. "You don't sound like you're from around here. Thought we'd halted all you dirty immigrants coming over here, stealing our jobs."

"Am not thief. Am mighty d—"

"Time for us to leave," I told Tali, stepping between her and the sneering man.

"Yeah, you do that, you dirty scum. Shit's hard enough as it is without bloody foreigners thinking they can —"

The man dropped to his knees as Tali gripped him by the throat and pulled her arm down. His face turned puce as he clawed at her bare arm, but Tali merely nibbled on her loaf and looked to me with questioning eyes.

"Should pull head off? Was rude. Not say nice things. Bad manners mean bad person. Maybe rip off arm? Teach lesson?"

"No, don't do that?" I hissed. "Let him go. You can't act like this. Everyone's watching."

"Maybe just chew off finger? Is nothing."

"Not even a finger."

"Must punish spiteful man. Charles always say is job. Eradicate nasty people."

"Yes, but only truly terrible ones. Not just rude people. Otherwise, there'd be hardly anyone left."

"Maybe would be better then," she said, fingers flexing.

"You might be right," I conceded, "but this isn't how we behave. Come on, let's go."

Tali glowered at the dying man, then released him. He curled up on the floor, gasping, as I nodded to the astonished baker who nevertheless winked at me and smiled before we turned and left the shop.

Outside, Charles beamed and chuckled, "That went better than I'd expected."

I shook my head, then admitted, "Yeah, me too. Good job, Tali. But next time, try not to kill anyone just for being rude."

"Why?" she asked, genuinely perplexed.

"Yeah, good question. Come on, time to go home. I think we've had more than enough action for one day."

"No, wait," said Charles. "Just one more thing before we go."

"Charles, she's exhausted. In case you've forgotten, we had an early start this morning."

"How could I forget? You keep reminding me. And you will get paid. You did a good thing. But look, how about we go over there? It will be good for Tali. Lots of practice."

"Absolutely not."

"Where go?"

"It doesn't matter," I told Tali. "Charles is just being mischievous. Wouldn't you rather go home and sleep? Maybe hunt on the way back?"

"Love to hunt."

"Or," said Charles, "we could see just how strong Tali is in her human form."

"Yes, do that. Tali is mighty dragon, stronger than all creatures."

"Charles, we haven't tested her strength," I hissed. "You think this is the best place to do it?"

"Oh, don't be such a spoilsport. I'm all for being discreet, but there's nobody around so I think we'll be fine. Come on. Live a little."

Charles beamed, then led us over to the market. At the end of the stalls was an old-fashioned carnival strength tester. The poor guy manning it was kicking at the road with a very scuffed boot, looking almost desperate for business. His face lit up when we approached.

"Ring the bell an' win a prize, mate. Simple."

"I bet you say that to everyone," said Charles curtly. "Anyone ever accomplished such a feat?"

"Course they 'ave. Loads of 'em." The elderly man's eyes shifted from us and focused on the stalls. It was an obvious ruse and as old as the fairground he'd clearly taken it from.

Nevertheless, Charles paid the man then handed the mallet to a confused Tali. "Just grip it tight, my dear, then thump that pad as hard as you are able. If the weight hits the bell, you win a prize."

"Is cheese?" she asked the owner.

"Is what cheese?"

"Prize?" Tali swung the mallet in front of her inexpertly, causing us to take a step back.

"No, it's a teddy bear, see?" He grinned as he held up a small teddy bear that had seen better days. Like thousands of them. Half an ear was missing, one eye was wonky, and I knew if I got close enough it would smell really bad.

"Is for Tali?" she asked, reaching out.

"You gotta ring the bell first," admonished the man. "But you ain't doin' it, are you? It's usually blokes wot 'ave a go."

"Tali can ring bell."

"Suit yourself." He shrugged.

Before anyone had the chance to show Tali how to grip the mallet properly, she hefted it above her shimmering head and slammed down so fast it would have been easy to miss. The bell dinged, then burst open the top of the contraption and soared at least fifty feet into the air.

We gasped as it reached its zenith then plummeted. Calm as you like, Tali cast the mallet aside, almost breaking the owner's knee-caps, reached out with her left hand, and caught the bell.

She handed it to the shocked man then asked, "Tali win teddy bear?"

Wordlessly, eyes wide, staring first at Tali then his ruined machine, he handed over the prize.

Tali inspected the bear, then ran her fingertips over the fake fur almost reverentially. "Is soft. Tali will keep."

"Sorry about the bell," I said lamely. "My friend here will pay for the damage. After all, it was his idea." I smirked at Charles, then went to catch Tali up as she wandered along the rows of stalls, taking no notice of all the looks she was getting from both men and women. She was, without doubt, the most stunning thing I think anyone had ever seen. It wasn't just the beautiful woman she had become, it was so much more than that. Her dragon nature somehow still managed to shine through.

She was proud, almost regal, but didn't act like she knew it. Sure, she held her head high, had great posture, but was unaware of just how arresting she was.

Charles caught us up and said, "At least now we know she can bash a few heads."

"We already knew that. Remember the state of your house?"

"Yes, yes, of course. I meant, she can use weapons when under pressure. Practice is never the same as real world experience. She maintained her human form when in the presence of strangers, and she learned that sometimes you can even win a prize."

"And eat a few loaves," I laughed.

Tali paused at a stall selling jewelry. The owner, a woman in her twenties with a plethora of tattoos and arresting blue hair, was explaining that she made them all herself and that they were imbued with magic.

"What magic? Can give Tali whispers?"

"Don't know what you mean, luv. What's whispers?"

"Is how do spells. Say magic words, make magic happen," Tali explained, surprisingly patient.

"Nah, they don't do none of that. It's inherent, see? I've got the witch in me, and when I make 'em, some of that gets passed on. Here, try this one. It'll suit your, er, coloring, and will hang nicely at your cleavage." The woman winked, eyes lingering.

Tali let the woman gather her hair behind her shoulders then fasten a delicate, simple teardrop silver pendant that hung between her arresting chest. The maker mussed Tali's hair so it looked even more incredible than ever, then directed the bemused dragon to the mirror.

"Looks incredible on you, luv. The silver really shows off your complexion. You're sparkling. And now you have a little bit of magic in you."

"Tali already has magic. Can morph and camouflage, make invisible to Necros, and even—"

"Yes, that's enough of that, I believe," said a flustered looking Charles as I watched, bemused, wondering how far he'd let it go.

"Say wrong thing?"

"Not at all, my dear. Actually, maybe. This fine lady doesn't want to hear about such things."

"Sorry. Forgot not supposed to tell. Head feel different."

I moved beside them and said, "You look very pretty. Would you like the pendant?"

"Is nice. Can still keep teddy bear?" Tali admired the bear she clutched tight in her hand as though afraid it would be stolen.

"Of course. Nobody's going to take it from you."

"Is mine to keep?"

"Yes, you won it. It's a prize. But I have to pay for the pendant."

"Allow me," said Charles.

"I got this. This is my gift to Tali. Her first piece of jewelry."

I paid the extortionate price, then we hurried away before the happy owner began talking about magic again.

Thank you for necklace. Is nice gift. Woman not tell truth about magic? Was lying?

She was lying, but not in a malicious or mean way. It's just what humans do sometimes. She wanted the sale, and thought saying the necklace and pendant were magical might make you buy it.

So was bad woman? Was wrong. Should punish like woman punish child?

No, it doesn't always work that way. She knew what she was doing, but wasn't being mean. Maybe she believed it would make it more exciting for you. And, if you like, I can give it some magic. A whisper just for you.

Tali stopped suddenly, and gripped my shoulders, our eyes level. "Make gift even more special?" she asked, fondling the pendant.

"Yes. To show how much you mean to me, and how proud I am of how you behaved today. And to say thank you for saving me. What whisper would you like?"

"Can turn into picture? When Tali touch pendant can make picture in Tali's head just for her?"

I thought of the many whispers I had learned over the years, then smiled and nodded as I found the perfect answer to her request.

Carefully, and as people passed us, I let the air around us compress a little, a barrier to the hubbub of the city, until it was just Tali and me, the rest of the world fading away.

I lifted the pendant carefully and let it rest in my palm, then spoke a gentle whisper, letting the words and power escape my lips. We watched as faint ribbons of my love for her trailed from my lips into the pendant. The elongated silver teardrop sparkled for a moment, then the whisper was done.

The sights, sounds, and smells of the market returned, crashing into us like a wave after such an intimate moment.

"Whisper worked?" asked Tali, eyes gleaming.

"Try it and see."

Eyes still locked on mine, the dragon eyes visible but only to me, Tali touched the pendant with her fingertips and gasped. "Can see Kifo and Tali at home, standing outside house. With Nava and Mai. And is warm. Is perfect picture. How took picture? This happened?"

"It's how you see your family. It's an image you created because of the whisper. So you'll always have something to remember us by, no matter what."

"Is perfect." Tali smiled coyly, then seemingly came to a decision and leaned forward and kissed me ever so lightly on my cheek. It almost stung, the sensation was so intense. A tingle that set my cheek on fire and clouded my mind.

I rubbed at the spot, then laughed and said, "That was a beautiful gift in return. Come on, we have one last treat for you. But Charles is buying," I warned him, knowing he'd been watching this whole incident with deep interest.

Tali moved ahead again, humming to herself as she swung her teddy bear, looking like she didn't have a care in the world.

"You don't know a whisper that can do that," chuckled Charles.

"No, but I put a little of my essence into the pendant, and that's better than any picture. Like I told her, she made her own image, one that means the most to her. It's the same thing," I shrugged.

"No, it's better. I'm proud of you. I'm proud of you both. She's incredible, isn't she?"

"She is, without doubt, utterly amazing."

We followed in Tali's wake, basking in her presence, unsurprised by the attention she received. She was like a movie star of old. People were awed by her presence, sensing there was something special about her but not quite able to figure out what. It went beyond her good looks, her regal bearing. There was just something more about her.

If only they knew how much.

Fish and Chips

Gasping horses and red-faced people trundled down roads, the streets sparsely populated as the afternoon sun rose to its zenith. Animals and humans alike vied for whatever shade they could find, keeping as close to the buildings as they were able. Arms and faces burned as, yet again, there was a shortage of sunscreen and the heat was too intense to cover up fully.

Tali was immune, and basking in the blistering heat. A pale goddess when all around were swarthy types like me with ruddy complexions and perpetually sunburned forearms. Charles was as unflappable as always, his two-tone brogues, freshly laundered suit and shirt incongruous, but he wore it with such confidence and a carefree attitude that he commanded respect. His fine half-elf features were better suited to a cold climate, yet he never seemed to burn or tan, just remained a warm golden hue that he carried off with aplomb.

Soon the hustle and bustle was replaced with an air of desperation and acceptance that life was a bitch and you didn't always get what you thought you deserved, just the scraps off your fellow man. We moved gratefully into the shade of an underpass where, in days gone by, vehicles would roar past overhead, their engines echoing off the damp, graffiti-covered supporting pillars. Now this was replaced with the growing numbers of dispossessed who made this place of lawlessness their home. Tarps, tents, ramshackle tin structures, you could find any type of makeshift building you could possibly imagine down here where no drones patrolled, no cameras watched, and nobody in authority ever ventured.

Charles greeted everyone with the same friendly wave and smile, unperturbed by his utter difference to them. But they didn't resent him, or certainly didn't show it if they did, as everyone understood he was something apart, and that he belonged here even if in a different role.

"People are happy?" asked Tali as she watched the homeless come and go.

"Some of them prefer the freedom this affords, others are barely hanging in there. It's the same whether you live in a house or not. But mostly people aren't happy. They want their freedom back. They want to travel, more than anything. Apart from food, of course. And that's why we're here. So you can get a little taste of what it's truly like to be human before we go home."

"And there's no finer example than Fishy Joes," beamed Charles as we stepped up to the mobile catering unit that hadn't been mobile for as long as anyone could remember.

"You better believe it," grinned Fishy Joe, his tanned, scrawny body belying the fact he lived in permanent shade and ran a fish and chips outlet single-handed.

"Is salmon? Tali like wriggly salmon."

"Even better," said Joe. "It's actual cod. The quotas are up this year and I've got an amazing supplier, so it's genuine cod today!"

"What is it usually?" I asked.

"Oh, er, you know, the other very high quality fish," mumbled Joe, then busied himself draining a batch of chips that were always crispy on the outside, soft and delicious inside, the same as the deep fried, battered "cod."

"Three portions and with mushy peas. Heavy on the salt and vinegar, light on the calories," declared Charles, almost salivating.

"You got it." Joe focused with his usual intensity on serving us our food while Tali watched intently.

"Joe, this is Tali. Tali, this is Joe," I said.

"How you coping, love? Bit of a big change for you, eh? Heard you got into some bother this morning, Kifo, and your day didn't get any better." Joe winked. "Charles, you should get better locks. I know a guy."

"How is it that you seem to know our business better than even I?" asked Charles. "I could do with someone like you on my team. I've never had a single informant as in the know as you, Joe, and it has always irked me how you won't divulge your source of knowledge."

"Just a guy trying to make a living," he laughed. "I hear things, is all."

"Joe knows about Tali?" she asked.

"Sure. You are a dragon. But I won't tell a soul, I swear. And nobody else knows. Top secret." Joe tapped a greasy finger to his large nose and winked.

"You exasperate me," sighed Charles. "And I am sure I don't need to tell you this is not to ever be discussed. I've killed men for knowing much less."

"Ah, but if you did that, who'd serve you such fine grub?" guffawed Joe as he slapped down three steaming cartons onto the spotless counter.

"True," Charles conceded, and I genuinely wondered if that was the reason why Joe remained alive. "What else do you know?"

"That you have a mission, that you showed the elves what for, and that you're all bloody insane. But thanks for stopping by. It means a lot to know you've come to me for your last supper."

"Way to boost our confidence," I grumbled.

"Last thing you all need is more confidence. But listen, be careful, and come home safe. I hope it works out for you. Poor guy deserves a break." Joe leaned forward and nodded over to the sole set of table and chairs where Shi was devouring his food eagerly.

"Thanks, and hopefully we'll see you again," I said.

We took our food and joined Shi at the rickety table. He grunted, looked up briefly, then resumed eating.

"That good, eh?" I chuckled.

"Bloody amazing. Joe's some kind of wizard."

"Put magic in food?" asked Tali, staring down at the now open trays.

"It's just a saying," said Shi between a mouthful. "It means it tastes so wonderful it's like it has magic in it."

"Sit, and taste," said Charles.

With practiced precision, Tali pulled the chair back, stood in front of it, then tried to simultaneously sit while moving the chair closer to the table. She ended up plonking down too far away, and frowned in consternation.

"You did really well," I said. "It's easy for us to forget that we've practiced sitting thousands of times. You'll get used to it."

"Human bodies so awkward. Is better to lie on ground. More natural. Why have chairs?"

"Lots of countries hardly use them. But here, where the ground is often wet, or was, it's a way of staying dry. Plus, it's easier to get up. But please, try the food," said Charles.

Keen to tuck in, we nevertheless waited while Tali picked up a chip and bit the end off. Her eyes widened, her tongue poked out, and she chewed slowly. Next, she tore off a chunk of battered cod and stuffed the oversized portion in her mouth then munched frantically. She swallowed, then smiled, cute dimples making her look even more adorable.

"Is good. Food taste different. More flavor. Mouth is different when human?"

"You have more taste buds," I explained. "When a dragon, your other senses are better than a human's, although you still retain most of it, but this is one sense that actually gets better. Along with touch." I flushed a little as I recalled her kiss and how electrifying it had felt.

"Tali likes."

Much to Charles' consternation and Shi's and my amusement, Tali tore into her fish supper with unabashed savagery. With her face practically in the food, she stuffed it in as fast as she was able to swallow, then when finished she wiped her glistening mouth with the back of her hand and leaned back with a satisfied sigh.

"I take it you enjoyed that?" I laughed.

"Tali like fish and chips. Prefer raw fish and like the wriggle, but when human will eat cooked."

"That's good to know," I said, keeping serious as I didn't want her to think she was being mocked.

Once we were finished, we returned the packaging to Joe who sorted everything into the various bins for either composting, recycling, or reuse, then left the strange, almost subterranean zone and emerged back into ferocious heat. Tali sighed with contentment when the sunlight bounced off her skin.

We wandered for a while, then Tali stumbled, unable to hold her form much longer. She'd managed several hours now, her record, and although nowhere near what we'd hoped, it would have to be enough for our mission. Every day we put this off increased the risk, so we had to do this, ready or not.

Finally, we made it back to the house, and Charles tentatively opened the front door.

"Wow, they're miracle workers," noted Shi as we entered to discover the cleaners had been and the house had resumed its cold, clinical look and feel.

"I preferred it with a bit of color," I sighed, hating how it felt in here.

"Blood is not conducive to a meditative experience," noted Charles as he checked the kitchen and grunted in satisfaction after inspecting the sink and tap.

"Need go home," said Tali. "Can go now?" Her form shifted, a hint of the dragon, then she dashed for the door.

"Meet you there?" I asked Charles.

"Let me just lock up and gather a few things, then I will come outside."

Shi and I joined Tali, who had already resumed her natural form, groaning with contentment as she swished her tail and rotated her neck to revel in her true essence.

"Will morph home. Kifo and Shi will come?" asked Tali.

"Are you sure you can?" I asked. "With both of us after such a tiring day?"

"Have energy. Fish and chips make strong." Tali snorted smoke then yawned, affording us a glimpse of the fire constantly burning within.

It was so incongruous, so beyond strange that mere moments ago she was a woman, now she was this magnificent creature, that my head swam with the craziness of such a thing.

"Then let's morph home."

"Guess I'll have to do the same," said Charles.

"I guess."

Charles was gone.

We mounted Tali, Shi complaining as usual, then I took a deep breath, steeled myself for what was to come, and succumbed to the inevitable as we rose above the city and let our forms dissolve into the Necroverse.

I doubled over as we arrived home, annoyed to see Charles simply adjust his tie, seemingly unmoved by the morph. I felt sick, hurt all over, and was ravenous even after our dinner. But Charles, not so much. Maybe because he was half-elf, maybe because of his prowess as a magic user, or maybe just because he was such a smug git there was no way he'd let anyone know he was hurting.

Shi and I slid off, stifling shrieks of pained discomfort, and watched as Tali stumbled over to the house. She looked back at me, tapped the pendant—that somehow still hung around her neck—gently with a talon, and smiled as she pictured the image she'd chosen. Then her eyelids drooped, she curled up outside the house, her teddy clutched under one leg, and fell asleep.

"Aw, so sweet," cooed Charles.

"It is," I admitted. "I forgot about the necklace. How does it still fit her?"

"Because she is a dragon with more magic than we could ever hope to muster. And because she wishes to keep the gift."

"She sure likes that teddy too," I noted.

"Never forget, sometimes she is like a child. She did well today. Much better than expected."

"She did amazing. There's so much for her to learn."

"And that will never end if she wishes to be your mate."

"I don't think that's a good idea."

"Don't be ridiculous. I know you well enough to know when you are lying even to yourself."

"You saw her. It's too much for her. She's a dragon."

"She is more than that. She is your dragon and you are her human. You can't fight your destiny, my dear boy. You should know that by now. Come, we have much to discuss."

"Haven't we gone over it all already?" I whined.

"Yes, and no. There is much I have told you, yet more I have not."

"For fuck's sake, Charles, don't say that like it surprises me. You never tell me what's going on. I can't believe we're bloody related."

"My dear boy, sometimes neither can I. Or that Shi is my son. What a truly peculiar world this is."

Charles headed for the house. I had little choice but to join him. The more information I got about this looming trip, the better. If not for my sake, then for Tali's. That little display today was nothing compared to what she would have to do if we were all to make it back out of the elven homeworld alive.

Nava returned with a bloody muzzle and a very extended tummy. He smiled when he saw us and dashed over, then slowed with a groan and more waddled than ran.

"I'm guessing the hunting was good today?" I asked as I rubbed his bristly fur.

"The rabbits are getting brave. Now there are a few less. I might have overdone it."

"Then go rest, as we have a very busy day tomorrow. I take it you still want to come?"

"Of course. You need me, and I wouldn't miss out on seeing how the elves live. And maybe if I get to bathe too, I won't have this old leg injury. Will the water heal it, Charles?"

"Absolutely. But Kifo is right, you should rest. Let your meal digest, and be sure to have an empty stomach tomorrow. We will take provisions, but going through the portal with a stomach like yours will not end well for you or any of us."

"Then it's a good thing I hunted today." Nava sniffed my legs then noted, "You smell like vampire. Did you have fun without me?"

"We might have come up against some rather hostile intruders."

"And Tali helped?"

"How can you tell?"

"Because you aren't covered in bite marks," he laughed, then sidled over to Tali and wedged himself against her flank.

Shi joined us just as the door was flung open and Mai pelted out, the door slamming shut behind him.

"Get ready for a bollocking," groaned Shi, eyes darting for an escape route.

"Man up and take your punishment. And at least it means you'll have clean clothes for tomorrow," I said.

"I have a change of clothes in the house," he whined, and then it was too late.

"Look at you both!" Mai tutted. "What a mess. Why can't you be more like Charles and me and at least remain semi-presentable?"

"Is that what you think of me, Mai?" asked Charles kindly. For some reason, they both seemed to adore one another, and Charles always got a nice cuddle.

"You look marvelous as always," said Mai as he hugged Charles' leg.

Charles bent and scooped up the wriggling house gnome. They embraced, shared a private whispered joke, then he lowered Mai who turned to us with a scowl.

"Get your clothes off and don't you dare touch anything with those greasy fingers. A shower, then Mai will make coffee. But only for good boys, not dirty ones."

"Yes Mai," Shi and I chorused, not even bothering to argue. We dutifully stripped to our underwear, much to Charles' amusement, then plodded into the house where we handed our bundled clothes to a waiting Mai, his foot tapping impatiently.

"Shower," he ordered, pointing to the bathroom.

"Yes Mai," we giggled, then he left us, tutting as he went.

"He's so great," chuckled Shi.

"He is. The place wouldn't be the same without him around."

"How'd you meet? How come he's here?"

"Let's get clean, then I'll tell you over coffee."

"It's quite the story," said Charles, studying us both, his good humor fading as he took in our bodies. "I'm sorry. Look at you both. What a mess. And before you say anything, yes, you both have great muscles and look very strong and manly, but that's not what I meant. So many scars. So many battles. So much death."

"And yet we're still standing," I said. "You gave us that. You gave us the option, and this is what we chose. Charles, I know I'm not a regular man. I understand that I am a Necro, but an incredibly lucky one. I don't get the Necronotes like most of our kind do, and am blessed in so many other ways. Yes, bad shit happened, still does, but I do good. I assassinate evil people, which gives me purpose in this crazy thing we call life. I heal quickly from these wounds, and it's the price I pay."

"Same," said Shi with a shrug. "I know I was a right handful when a kid, but you stuck with it and did what you could. You taught me everything I needed to know, and always stood by me even when I did the most terrible thing imaginable. I earned these scars. Yes, mine are mostly because of the notes, and because of my shifter nature, but all of us have wounds. It's just ours are more visible than most. I've already lived longer than nearly every other human who has ever existed, and I accept this is the price to be paid. Don't beat yourself up. You did good."

"Boys, you don't know how much that means to me. I'm speechless." Charles let his tears flow. There was no shame. He embraced us both and didn't let us go for the longest time.

A Little Story

"Mai has made coffee," he sang out as he stumbled across the clearing, regained his footing, then hurried over to where we huddled by a small fire. We didn't need the heat, but Nava liked it, and it gave us a focal point to sit around.

"Thank you, Mai," I said as I took the tray from him and placed it on a stump. "Will you join us? I was about to tell Shi how you came to be here with me. Or maybe you would prefer to tell the story? Would you like a small coffee?"

"Mai can have coffee?"

"Yes, but a very little one. Why don't you grab your cup?"

We watched an excited Mai scurry off to the house to retrieve his personal cup. He wouldn't drink from anything else as he said it was the only one he knew for certain was always clean. What that said about the others, I never had quite figured out.

"What's with the coffee thing?" asked Shi, taking his mug with a nod.

"I'm sure you've noticed Mai is rather highly strung? Quite manic at times?"

"Yeah, hard to miss."

"And smaller than us?"

"Up to my knees. He's a gnome."

"So stimulants are much more potent if he takes a human dose. He once drank a tumbler of this rancid moonshine I suffered my way through and got so drunk he cleaned the entire forest."

"Very funny," chuckled Shi, then turned to Charles when neither of us laughed.

Charles nodded. "It was spotless. He even arranged all the pine needles by size. We found thirty squirrels sitting beside a pyramid of pine cones. They couldn't move. Somehow, he'd mesmerized them and graded them by color."

"The pine cones?"

"No, the squirrels. The whole sorry incident took him days, and when he sobered up he didn't remember a thing."

"If he drinks too much coffee, he's even worse. He gets beyond manic, won't stop, and talks so fast it's impossible to understand him. I think he reverts to his native tongue, but it's hard to tell."

"So if he gets wasted or full of caffeine he goes on a cleaning frenzy? Sounds like you'd always keep a bottle in," Shi grinned.

"He's rather OCD, so the last thing I need is him obsessing about things even more. You've seen what he's like. He's such a great guy. I don't want him becoming addicted."

"Hello," said Mai as he returned with his cup. "I made it," he said, puffing out his chest as he showed Shi.

"That's, er, an interesting shape. Nice work."

"Thank you." Mai beamed as he poured himself a half cup of coffee into the weird blob-like vessel with a crooked handle and a wonky bottom he took immense pride in showing off. He sampled his coffee and sighed. "Ah, how wonderful! I haven't tasted it for a long time. Mai must be careful with human drugs, or things can go wrong. I still have dreams about squirrels!"

"You'll be fine with that, as long as you stay off the hard stuff."

"I will," he said, nodding vigorously.

"Shi wanted to know how we came to live together. Shall I tell him?"

"Yes, and I will interrupt when you get it wrong."

"Oh great," I laughed.

"So, once I was twenty-one and we realized that I wasn't going to receive my note, we, meaning I, figured it was best I got a place of my own. Charles found this cool spot here and bought it for me."

"I heard all about that. Very generous," said Shi.

"You could have had the same. Still can," noted Charles.

"Not now," Shi grumbled.

"And once I'd decided what I was going to build, I gathered the materials and got to work. I wanted to do it all, keep myself occupied and out of trouble if nothing else. I began work, but soon realized I was way out of my depth."

"You didn't get any builders in?" asked Shi, glancing at the house. "It's a bloody amazing place."

"Nope, it was just going to be me. Not even Charles was going to help."

"Although I offered many times," said Charles.

"But like I said, I soon realized building a house alone is a lot harder than you can imagine. I got so far, then became overwhelmed by the scale of the project."

"Silly boy," chuckled Mai as he sipped his coffee, foot already tapping as the caffeine kicked in.

"Very," I admitted. "One day, I was sitting out here, right in this spot actually, trying to explain to Tali how I wanted her to help lift the beams and hold them while I fixed them in place. It made no sense to her. She couldn't visualize what I meant, and the things she did help me with —" I glanced over to ensure she was sleeping, "—were beyond frustrating, as dragons aren't big into construction and she would snap more wood than she held."

"Tali is better at burning wood," said Mai with a smile.

"She sure is. Tali left for a nap and I was brooding, grumbling about things and generally feeling sorry for myself even though I'd created this mess."

"So Mai came to rescue Kifo from his own daft behavior!"

"You did. It was sweltering hot, I was soaked through with sweat, and had a pile of timber and nobody to help me. And then, right there in the fire pit, the earth began to shift. I assumed it was a mole that had been causing chaos on the vegetable plot, so grabbed my shovel and was about to whack it over the head when it popped up. I had the shovel raised, and waited, and then this head of wild hair emerged, followed by a friendly face, and Mai's nose twanged as it was pulled free from the hole. He clambered out, brushed himself down until his tunic and housecoat were spotless, and said he heard my request and would gladly be my house gnome once there was a house. He said he needed the position as his family had been distraught for centuries because he had nobody to care for. The rest, as they say, is history."

"A wonderful story," clapped Charles.

"Delightful," said Mai, then got to his feet and did a little jig.

"But where did you come from?" asked Shi, smiling.

"Home, of course. My old home."

"And where is that?"

"It's, er, where gnomes originate, silly." Mai resumed his seat, his entire body vibrating slightly as the coffee really took hold.

"And what happened with the house?" asked Shi.

"We built it!" Mai and I chorused, causing Nava to grumble then curl up into a tighter ball beside me.

"Did it take long?"

"It was very quick once Mai arrived," I said. "Mai knew all about building, and how to make the place homely but stylish, and the more we got to know each other, the faster the work went. He worked incredibly hard, and never complained."

"I did! I complained all the time," he sang happily.

"True," I laughed. "And so did I. But in just a few weeks, it went from a foundation and a pile of wood to the finished thing."

"Weeks?"

"Yes. Mai was a whirlwind. He worked tirelessly, and was so speedy that most of the day and a lot of the night he was nothing but a blur. I couldn't even attempt to keep up."

"Then well done to you, Mai," said Shi.

"Mai thanks you. It was my honor. And now Mai looks after the home and has his own true place in the world."

"We all need a place in the world," I agreed.

"Maybe," grumbled Shi.

"It doesn't have to be somewhere you live," I said hurriedly. "Just somewhere you know you are welcome. You always had that with Charles, and now you have it here, with us."

"Shi is always welcome at our home," agreed Mai. "He is family." With a nod, then a bow to each of us in turn, Mai retrieved his cup and whistled his way back to the house.

"He's such a nice fellow," said Charles with a genuine smile.

"He turned this place into a true home. I can't imagine what it would have been like without him. I know I'd still have Nava and Tali, but it wouldn't be the same."

"You got it made," said Shi. "I was hoping he'd give some insight into his homeworld, but he's like so many other races I've spoken to. The longer they're here, the less they recall, until the specifics fade away."

"It's the way of things. This is his home and shall remain that way for as long as Kifo lives. Even then, he may choose to stay and welcome a new owner. If they find each other suitable, then he will help them. If not, he will return to his original home."

"Do you know anything of the gnome homeworld? In fact, how about all of them? Where are they? I mean in space? Like, when we get to the elven homeworld—" Shi stood as he warmed to his subject, "—will there be different stars, different suns? Are they the other side of the universe, or in our galaxy or what? I've never understood any of it. Not that I've looked into it too deeply, mind. But I'm curious."

"The universe as a whole, it's very existence, is an utter mystery," said Charles. "Nothing but theories as to how it exists, what came before, and even how it functions. And those scientists aren't Necro, so their theories are based on assumptions we know to be wrong. We live in a world where magic is real. Where beings from other places can visit, even stay, and where our kind can shape-shift into other forms, defying the laws of physics as they deem to be true. Why should we understand where other races abide? It's not time for us to know, and maybe it never will be. But I can tell you this."

"Yes," we both asked eagerly.

"The elven homeworld is a place where magic truly does reside. Where the laws and rules are very different from ours. Yet it must be in the same universe, surely?"

"Why's that?" I asked.

"Because if it wasn't, how could we possibly go there?" said Charles, looking smug.

"That's not an answer," I complained.

"Utter crap," said Shi. "You don't know, so you're just making stuff up."

Charles laughed heartily. I knew by his relaxed manner that he was relishing this time we spent together, the same as Shi and me. It had been a good week as we slowly recovered and got to know one another, but this might be our last so it was great we were all here.

Our conversation carried on into the evening, where coffee was replaced with wine and beer. Nava slept through most of it, Mai came and went, always busy with one thing or another, and Tali left to hunt once dusk came, returning with a deer she set about devouring for hours, heeding Charles' warning about no food the following morning.

"Are you both ready for what awaits us?" asked Charles as he closed the book we'd fought so hard to keep.

"I am," said Shi.

"Me too."

Shi turned to me and said yet again, "You don't have to do this. I know we dragged you into it all and that's deceitful, but it's one hell of an ask. We shouldn't have treated you like that, but I didn't know what else to do. It was wrong, and I don't want to risk losing you now. Maybe you should stay behind? Yes, it's for the best. Stay, and we'll be back soon enough. Tali can just get us in there, we'll do what we need to, then be back in no time."

"Stop trying to talk yourself out of me coming. I said I would, and that I forgive you. I understand why you did what you did, and it's okay. I'm coming, and that's final."

"But we got you into that crap with the elves, fighting those dark mages, and you didn't have a clue why."

"It was to save Charles."

"Yes, but you didn't know what he was up to. I should have told you."

"And like you said, it might have risked everything. What if I'd got annoyed and left you to it?"

"Would you have?"

"No. I'd have been angry, but still helped. But I understand that you waited until the time was right to tell me. And let's face it. You won't stand a chance without me. You need me. You need me and Tali. The odds are better the more of us there are, so let's not discuss this any more. Charles, are you ready? You know what we're doing?"

"I am, and I do. I have it all mapped out. We shall go over things in the morning, then leave. Let's get some rest. Tomorrow will be a very long, and very exciting day."

I lay awake in my bed long into the night. Not because I was worried or stressed or even concerned. Dwelling on the future was like dwelling on the past—a fruitless exercise as nothing I could currently do would change either. Rather, I thought of Tali. How regardless of what she was, what she could become, she was special to me. Just like Nava, or Mai, or Charles, and now Shi.

But with Tali it was deeper. We shared our blood. We were bonded. I felt it like I felt the crisp, cool sheets on my skin. I smelled her as richly and with more depth than I could smell the lemon scent on my pillow.

Sleep well, my love. You will have a great adventure tomorrow. The elves are blessed to have you honor them with your visit.

Tali loves Kifo. Will protect him. Are scared?

Never. Not with you by my side.

Is good we go. Help Shi. Is important.

Yes, it is.

Tali has father?

Every living thing has a mother and a father, remember?

Yes, Tali knows, but not knows. Does not feel presence of parents like feels presence always of Kifo. Why?

Because you weren't raised by them. For you, there is no memory of them. You emerged from your egg to save me. You heeded my call and you burst from your shell and let the magic flow into me. We are the same. I sometimes believe I was inside that egg with you. Does that make sense?

Tali was suddenly very animated in my head, her emotions swirling excitedly. *Kifo feels same as Tali! Know not happen, but feels like we came from egg at same time.*

Maybe we did, and this is all a dream.

Tali never dream.

No, you don't need to dream.

Why?

Because you are perfect the way you are. Your mind has no issues to resolve while you sleep. You are already exactly what you were meant to be.

Tali yawned, and I felt her tiredness, and then she slept.

For the first time in many months, I had a dreamless sleep too. When I woke up, it was to my worst nightmare.

House guests.

Time to Leave

Mai was screaming at Shi for leaving a wet towel on the floor, Nava was barking excitedly as Charles adjusted his shirt sleeves, and then Tali burst the door open and her head craned in, eyes alert for danger.

"It's okay, it's just our guests being very noisy," I told her. For a moment, I thought she might try to enter in dragon form, but luckily she was satisfied with my answer after checking the room and retreated with a nod.

"I didn't make a sound," said Charles.

"Neither did I," groaned Shi as he tugged on his t-shirt over damp hair and ignored Mai tutting about water spots on the floorboards.

"Someone was making a right commotion," I grumbled, then realized I was stark naked so hurried to my bedroom to dress.

When I returned, it was to a wonderful aroma of coffee. My coffee. The last of my coffee, I suspected.

I sat at the old table in my sparse kitchen and grunted as I sipped the precious nectar.

"Are you in a bad mood?" asked Charles.

"I think I am," I admitted. "I'm not good with company for so long. I'm not used to it."

"Oh, thank fuck for that," blurted Shi, then cast his eyes down.

"What?"

"No offense, but it's driving me nuts living here. I thought you wanted me here, which is why I hung around."

"No, I wish you'd bugger off and just visit now and then."

"That's great!" said Shi, banging his mug on the table and spilling coffee. Mai was on it in a flash, standing on the table whilst wiping away the mess and tutting. Shi leaned sideways to talk past him and asked, "You didn't want me to stay? You said I should."

"I was being polite. I knew you were exhausted, and hurt, and what with everything that happened, I assumed you wanted to spend time with me."

"I did. I do. But I'd rather sleep outside and meet up in the afternoons or something. It's been a bitch of a week, mate. I can't relax with these smells of lemons and pine and the itchy sheets."

Charles and I recoiled as the air became a vacuum, all sound sucked into the void. Mai began to shake, fists bunched, and stepped forward until his long rubbery nose touched Shi's. "Did you just say my sheets were itchy? How dare you! I've never been so insulted in my life."

"Then you should get out more," snapped Shi, then slapped a hand over his mouth as he realized what he'd said. "Sorry, didn't mean that. And Mai, your sheets are divine. Too nice for the likes of me. What I meant is I'm not used to using sheets. I sleep under trees in my sleeping bag, or just my clothes. I don't do house stuff."

Mai glared hard at Shi, then hopped off the table and muttered while he rinsed out the cloth into a bucket I swear wasn't there a moment ago.

Charles and I shook our heads at Shi, who grinned cheesily and asked, "So you want your peace back?"

"Yes please. You don't mind? Really?"

"No, I get it. I'm used to being alone, too. What about this weird guy?" Shi indicated Charles with his thumb. "He's been hanging around like he hasn't got a home to go to."

"A lot," I grumbled, but smiled at this enigmatic man.

"My dear boys, believe me when I say that I love you both, but that you have been driving me absolutely crazy."

"Us?" we chorused.

"Yes. Your foul language is offensive to my ears. Your manner of speaking is bizarre and —"

"At least we don't say things like 'dear boy' and talk like we're in English class," I laughed.

"You sound like you're an aristocrat from the nineteen fifties. One of those old TV broadcasters where everyone had the same posh accent," said Shi, nudging me and winking.

"A byproduct of my upbringing and the circles I was forced to mix in. Of course, when I was a lad, speech was very different, words too, but as things evolved, I moved with the times, yet never seemed to quite get to grips with modern parlance."

"There you go again. Who says 'modern parlance' these days?" Shi chuckled.

"You say 'mate,' even to me and Charles," I reminded him.

"Yeah, well, guess we all have our quirks of speech. You pick up lots of modern slang, but there's this history you can't shake. You're lucky being so young. Makes you sound like you belong. Me and Charles not so much."

"Can we please get back to the point?" I asked.

"As I was saying before being interrupted," said Charles with a frown to Shi, "I have only been around so much because this family dynamic is new to us all. We needed time to get to know one another again, to bond now there are the three of us. And it has been glorious. Shi, I have missed you so much, and feel desolate that we haven't spent more than a handful of hours together in decades. It isn't right. And you two have only known each other a matter of days. I wanted to be here to ensure you got along."

"We get along," I said.

"Of course you do, but it was still a risk. And we have Tali to think of. After her incident, I thought it best to be close by, just in case. But all is well, and now I will resume my normal duty, but I promise I will be a better father, a better grandfather, and we must get together more often."

"You were a great father-figure to me," I said. "You did a fantastic job and were always there for me. I owe you everything, Charles."

"Me too," agreed Shi. "You raised not only me, but Kifo too. And you didn't get him involved in Eloise's crap, which I find incredible."

"She has never been happy about that," said Charles, shuddering at what were clearly some bad memories.

"What did she have to say about all this?" asked Shi, knuckles white as he gripped his mug.

"Why do you care?" I asked.

"It's complicated. But she's family, and powerful, and a pain in the ass."

"Eloise has, rather surprisingly, been nothing but supportive. She offered her assistance, she offered her protection, and she offered her best wishes to you both. She even agreed not to interfere in our little quest, which I find highly suspicious."

"Yeah, very," grumbled Shi. "What does she want out of this? She always wants something."

"Just information. I gave her the highlights of this book we have, and provided her with copies of the maps, and I promised to tell her what we uncovered. But beyond that, she wants nothing but for it to be a success. I must remind you, Shi, that after what happened twenty-seven years ago and Kifo was left without a mother, your stuck-up, pompous, manipulative great-aunt promised to do all in her power to help you. It was you who eschewed our assistance, our love, and remained apart from your family. I am not judging you, I understand completely, but she stuck by you."

"But only because it was in her own self-interest." Shi's face hardened, but he kept his voice low and calm.

"To a degree, yes. Everything is. But she promised to help when the time came and we could obtain a brooch. She provided money, if that was what we required, and never asked for anything in return. I work for her because it suits me, not because she insists or even asked. I am my own man, as are you both, but she is family."

"What exactly does she do?" I wondered, not for the first time.

"She helps keep our world a little safer. She works for nobody, answers to nobody as far as I can tell, and has more money than is right or proper."

"And flaunts it," Shi reminded him.

"Yes, well, that's a discussion for another day. Remember, her upbringing was different to yours, even mine, and we aren't communists yet. Some have more, others have less. Yes, she is an extreme example, but she remains living in her godawful house in that street overrun with all that's worst about society, and she does so not only because of sentiment, but because she remains at the heart of the problems this country faces."

"And has enough manpower to protect herself."

"Indeed. That goes without saying. What she does do very well is uncover those who would destroy our Necro culture, our very way of life, and does what she can to prevent the government or more important players in how the world functions from pushing things too far. And before you ask, yes, she has her own agenda. Don't we all? But she tries to do what is right for our country, helps turn the tide of this current madness we are involved in under the pretense of saving the planet and us. Things have gone too far, we have no freedom, and she abhors tyranny even though she is the epitome of a tyrant herself. As I have said before, it is a complicated matter."

"What does she actually do to help, though?" I asked, pushing it.

"She helps those she has an affinity with succeed. Get into government, be able to change the laws. She knows judges, high-ranking members of the police, army, things like that. Over time, she has made a difference. Not that you'd know it, but you don't realize what this country would have been like otherwise. She is, when all is said and done, just one woman with a very stubborn attitude. She doesn't make the rules, and I'm thankful for that, but she tries to do right by us in her own rather pompous, self-entitled way. And she's family. She raised me and was like a mother to me. She is a good woman and I love her. We all have our faults, but she stood by me and never once forced me into anything. I owe her everything, and that means so do you two. Without her, none of us would be alive."

"And on that note, how about we get this damn day started?" I said, sick of hearing about Eloise and what she may or may not be involved in. I decided a long time ago that I wanted nothing to do with politics or law-making. I had neither the patience nor the stomach for such a world.

"Yes, shoo," cooed Mai with rather too much glee. He hopped onto the table and looked at each of us in turn, inspecting us for signs of dirt, no doubt. "Outside with you boys now. Mai has much to do and you are making a mess. I will see you all later, so fare thee well and hurry home. Do not," he warned, "get blood on your clothes. Although, I suppose I'm certain you will. Oh, what is a poor house gnome to do with such messy men?"

"We'll try our best to stay clean," I told him.

"Thank you, Kifo. Be safe." Mai hugged me, then the others, and wiped a tear from his eye before straightening his housecoat and whipping out the duster to hide his concern.

With no reason to remain inside, I grabbed Ziggy, slid him into the leather holster at my belt that was as magical as the weapon itself, and could accommodate Ziggy in any reasonable size or shape, and put my boots on.

Charles and Shi joined me. Shi with his sword strapped to his back, dark jeans and shirt matching his hair, his rugged face making him look every ounce the assassin, much like me, and I realized how similar we looked.

Charles was suited and, amazingly, booted, but he managed to carry it off with panache. He had a wicked knife in a holster hidden by his suit jacket, and most likely several other weapons concealed about his person, both magical and not, and one other very important item. The book with the maps.

We gathered at a rickety picnic bench and called for Nava and Tali to join us.

"Is everyone ready?" asked Charles.

We reluctantly agreed we were. "Good. Now, we all know the plan?" We nodded. "Let's go over it one more time. Just to be sure." Everyone groaned.

"Tali know plan. Go through portal in middle so everyone close to Tali and not go funny in head. Will be by big water. Everyone but Tali go in and get wet. Be healed of problems. Come back through portal. Have nice lunch."

"Lunch sounds amazing," I groaned, my stomach rumbling.

"You're hungry?" asked Charles, shocked.

"I could eat," I admitted.

Everyone else said they could too.

"Don't forget," said Charles, "we must only go into the water at the edge. It is imperative we stay near to Tali. Without the dragon's power, we will be unable to think coherently, become extremely ill, the pain will be nigh on unbearable, and we may well die. Do not go anywhere without Tali." He turned to her and said, "We will emerge with you as a woman, and please stay in human form. This is very important, Tali. You cannot be a large dragon there. You will be seen or sensed easily, and then we will have untold problems. Remember what we practiced, and try to behave as a woman should. If the rest of us are discovered, then we may be able to bluff our way out for a while thanks to the new whispers we have learned that will disguise our appearance, but we cannot hide a massive dragon."

"Tali knows. Will be pretty woman and can adjust ears to look pointy like silly elf. Is good."

"Nava, be sure to stay close to us. We aren't sure what effect the place will have on you, and could find no information, so the first sign of anything feeling odd, get as close as you can to Tali," I reminded him.

"I'm not planning on going anywhere without her. I'll be in the water then straight back out, and you should all do the same."

"We will," said Charles. "If we get this right, and my calculations indicate we will, we will be gone for a mere matter of minutes. But remember, and this is the most important thing, the brooch that creates the portal only works once a year, and for a day. If we don't get back within twenty-four hours, we are stuck. For good. Not that I expect we could hold out, even with Tali, for an entire day. So let's be quick, let's be discreet, and let's get going."

"Does anyone need to do anything before we go?" I asked.

Tali does, she said into my head. *Kifo will not be cross?*
With you? Never.
Was cross before.
When?
Was lost to blood of witch. Kifo said never look at him in that way or would not be bonded.
That was different. You scared me. You must never scare me. But that was one time.
Am sorry.
I know you are. It's in the past.
Happy. Will fetch best thing.

Tali turned and approached the house, and I understood what she wished to do. I told the others, "No laughing, and no arguing about this. Our world is confusing enough without Tali thinking you're making fun of her."

Both men nodded, and we watched as Tali shape-shifted into her human form then bent and retrieved her prize from yesterday. She drifted back over, face solemn, the new pendant glinting in the morning light pushing between the forest canopy.

"Can take Bear?"

"Of course," said Charles. "Is that its name? Bear?"

Tali nodded, and I caught a glimpse of her elven ears, something we'd practiced hard to get right. "Is nice name?" She stroked the raggedy bear's head as though it were a dog, then held it out and smiled. "Is good luck charm. And most precious gift bring luck too." She fondled the teardrop pendant and was lost to the image it brought forth for a moment before casting her gaze on us.

"A very good name," said Shi. "And you have your present from Kifo too, so you're all set."

"One more thing," noted Charles. "Tali, don't forget your eyes. They are as beautiful and arresting as ever, but remember what we said? They should be blue like an elf's for our trip."

With a nod, Tali's eyes became as pale and piercing as my own.

"So let's do this," I said. "We'll arrive just back from the water's edge on a shallow bank leading to the lake. It's surrounded by trees and there shouldn't be anyone about as there's no road access. It looks like the elves use the other side, so this should be easy."

We moved excitedly to the middle of the compound with plenty of space around us, then Charles pocketed the book he'd sealed in a slim metal case to protect from water, fire, and more importantly any magic. As a deep silence descended, he slid the ornate silver brooch resembling an eye on its side reverentially from a leather pouch and held it out in front of him.

"Ready?"

Everyone nodded. Shi shifted nervously, Tali was calm, Nava rubbed against my leg.

Charles pressed his thumb into the opaque, pale precious stone in the center of the brooch and it glowed red.

The portal was opened.

Bad Start

A pinprick of silver light appeared with a mini implosion, sound vanishing for a moment, then everything whooshed back in and the birds resumed their chorus.

The portal, what I could only think of as an eye, expanded. Energy crackled around the outer perimeter like fire as it quickly grew and offered a glimpse out into a familiar yet otherworldly scene.

I knew Charles was keeping a sharp mental image of the map he'd acquired, opening the portal exactly where we wished to be, and he was already sweating under the immense mental power it must have been taking. If he wasn't half-elf, I doubted he would have been able to accomplish such a feat.

Pale, perfect, blue-tinted water was as calm as glass. The sun, or *a* sun, shone down on the strange water, silver glinting off any slight imperfections of the placid lake. Far on the other side, a long stretch of sandy beach ran for at least a mile in each direction. Trees clung to the steep sides of a cliff where waterfalls tumbled over flower-laden crevices. Behind the valley walls, astonishingly beautiful mountains rose to unfathomable heights in the far distance, capped with snow and bizarrely shaped clouds that bore little resemblance to anything I'd ever witnessed. Trees were the wrong color, grass in both green and purple hues, and magisterial buildings with large pillars supporting vast verandas glinted under the alien sun.

Charles nodded to us, then we took our positions. Nava led, then Charles, then Tali. I was right behind her, with Shi bringing up the rear.

Once Charles was through, the portal would begin to close, so we had scant seconds to make it.

Not knowing if the portal would bend to his will, we had decided on the single-file approach for entering, but the portal seemingly obeyed and widened, affording us the option to walk through simultaneously. We spread out into our new formation, then stepped through into a truly alien environment.

The world constricted around me. I was falling, vaguely aware of screams. One was my own as I sucked in alien air then slammed into water feet first and sank below the surface of Lake Elinor. Sight and sound vanished as the shock of the portal dumping us into the lake confounded my senses. My eyes snapped open, but they stung as the foreign liquid washed away my tears, leaving me with nothing but blurred vision and a sense of disoriented helplessness. Nevertheless, I forced them to remain open as I knew otherwise I would have no chance of finding the others if they failed to emerge from this potentially watery grave.

Vision remained extremely poor, the water clear but still too much for my eyes, and I saw nothing but a blur. Steeling myself for what I knew I must do, I sank lower, my lungs already burning, then hit the bottom and let my legs bend before pressing against the sandy lake bed and pushing up. Forcing panic down, I kept my arms rigid by my sides to streamline my form and shot upward, gasping as my head emerged into the elven air.

I trod water, spinning to find that Charles had already surfaced. Shi popped up next to him, spluttering as he attempted to brush aside the hair covering his face, and Nava almost propelled out of the water before paddling over to me.

"Where's Tali?" he panted, eyes darting.

"I don't know. I can't see anything down there. We have to find her. Damn, she can't be in water. And she sure as shit can't swim. She's never even got wet before." In my panic, I ducked under and got a mouthful of the lake, the taste sweet yet bitter at the same time. Hacking out the water, I took a deep breath then followed Nava back under to search for Tali.

My boots weighed me down enough to stay submerged, but the weight, and my t-shirt riding up and billowing made swimming difficult. I floundered and spun, searching with cloudy eyes for Tali. Nava brushed past me, streamlined and proficient underwater, and he barked, the sound peculiar. I followed him as he dove to the bottom. He shook his head, indicating he had been mistaken, then darted up for air. I spun, frantic, but Tali was nowhere to be seen. Sickness threatened to overwhelm me, and I knew I couldn't hold out much longer without her close by my side, but there was no choice apart from to keep going until the very end.

I swam awkwardly to the surface and sucked in air before nodding to Nava and we dove back under. We spun circles, then swam out deep into the lake, our movements erratic, co-ordination weakening every second. My head pounded, my muscles screamed, and I felt my life draining away. We weren't meant to be here, we couldn't be here, and without Tali's presence, death would claim us soon enough.

Nava barked, and I used every ounce of my remaining energy to reach him. He dove and I followed. We found Tali on her back on the very bottom. Her eyes were wide open, but there was no life there.

My world collapsed around me.

She couldn't be gone.
Not Tali. Not her.
Not my beloved.

The dire warnings of being apart from the dragon in the elven world crashed into me with renewed force as pain engulfed me. My thoughts clouded, every nerve alight, and movement became almost unbearable. But I forged on, and pushed against the water until I snagged her hand and began to swim awkwardly for the surface with my lungs fit to burst.

Nava shunted her from behind, clearly not in as much discomfort as me, but certainly feeling the separation from what allowed us to enter this place.

With my face clear of the water, I coughed up what felt like an entire lake then called out for Charles and Shi. Where were they? Had they already drowned? I searched everywhere as I trod water, but saw nothing. A moment later they surfaced, spluttering and calling out that they couldn't find her.

"I have her," I called hoarsely, "but she drowned. Hurry up, we need to get her out of here. She's dead. Dead!"

Charles and Shi swam in a panic, awkward and uncoordinated as the strange environment took all they had.

"Grab her other arm," I told Shi. "Charles, cradle her head. We have to get her to shore. There might still be time."

Nava pushed her feet while we swam, every stroke torture, thoughts becoming more incoherent by the second, but the sense of loss and the emptiness inside me was much worse than anything this world could throw at me.

We reached the shallows and gained our footing, then stumbled and slipped until we managed to drag her onto a shale and sand beach out of the clutches of the lake. All of us were shaking uncontrollably, hardly able to breathe as our organs began to shut down, but we wouldn't give in to it. We couldn't.

Tali wasn't breathing, and her skin was as pale as the sand, but she was still warm. As my tears fell, I held on to that as I would not accept she was gone from my universe. She was my universe, I realized. My reason for being. Strange, complicated, always loving in her own way, this creature was my salvation. She clutched Bear in rigid fingers, her pendant hung to the side, half-buried in the coarse sand.

"Move aside," snapped Charles, crawling around her then straddling her. With shaking hands, and as Nava whined and Shi clutched his head in agony as the loss of Tali began to take our minds as well as our ability to function, Charles prized open Tali's mouth and breathed raggedly between her beautiful lips.

He made erratic chest compressions, unable to get the rhythm just right, and then repeated mouth-to-mouth followed by more chest compressions. Water pumped from her lungs as he pressed forcibly on her ribcage, his face reddening under the strain of trying to resuscitate a body tougher than any human's.

Again, and again, the water burst from her mouth, but she didn't breathe.

Charles collapsed onto the sand, unable to hold himself upright, and clawed at his head as his mind began to unravel. Nava nipped at my boots, unable to control animal instincts as he tried to fight off unseen foes.

Every single movement I made was abject agony, but I would not let my beloved Tali perish in this fucking place so far from our home. I wriggled and clawed my way onto her body, felt the warmth of her flesh even as my senses shut down. My vision clouded and I had to track up her body with my hands to find her mouth. Gasping and screaming, I arched forward, and with cupped hands to make a seal I expunged what air I could hold in my lungs into her own, inflating them.

Her lips were so warm, I couldn't accept she was gone. Tali's body felt like it was burning up, but I was shaking so badly I couldn't tell if it was her or a fever. My skin tingled at the closeness, a fuzzy sensation that was almost pleasant for a brief moment, but then it turned sour and bitter and corrupt as unimaginable agony pounded in my head. I convulsed as I banged on her chest with my fist, railing against the fact I was unable to coordinate enough to perform correct compressions.

Five times I pounded, then, utterly blind now, screaming and throat burning from the water and the grief, I gave her my air again.

How long had it been? How long could she be gone before resuscitation wasn't an option? Did the rules for humans even apply to a dragon? And what about the fact she'd drowned? Dragons weren't meant to go near water, they never drank, so what did all this mean? Was this it? She was gone?

"No!" I bellowed, then with a raspy whisper I sobbed into her chest, "No, you can't. It's you and me against this fucked-up world, Tali. Come back."

Something gripped the back of my neck in an icy, tight hold and I wailed with soaring joy as I felt the steady pounding of her heart next to mine. Vaguely, as if from far away, I was aware of Charles bawling. Nava whined beside me. Shi mewled like a babe that had lost its mother.

Tali shot upright, her forehead smashing into my nose, cracking cartilage and sending a shooting pain into my head that was pure joy because it meant one thing.

She was alive!

I tumbled aside, smiling up at the alien sky as I shed tears of joy and coughed my way back to a reality I figured I could cope with now she was by my side.

Tali purged the remaining water with raspy coughs and violent urging, but all I heard was the sound of my own blood pounding in my head. The moment I was able, I got to my knees and as the others knelt to check on her too, I smiled at her and said, "You scared me. How are you?"

"Kifo's voice sound funny. Raw. Tali's too?" she asked, frowning, raising her hand to her throat.

"You had an accident. You drowned. We brought you back. But it was a close thing."

"Tali cannot die," she chided, smiling at me. "Am dragon."

"Not at the moment, you aren't. And you aren't at home, either. Maybe you can't die by any other means even here. I'm not sure of anything anymore. But you were in the water, and water and dragons, even shifter dragons, definitely don't mix."

"Was in water?" she asked, still suspicious.

"Yes. We all were. You fell in and sank. We got you out, but you weren't breathing. You were dead. Charles tried to bring you back but couldn't, so I tried and you did it! You came back to life."

"Kifo saved Tali like she saved him long ago?" she asked, clutching at my soaked shirt.

"It wasn't quite as spectacular, and I think Charles did most of the work," I admitted.

"No, I couldn't resuscitate her," rasped Charles. "It was your connection that saved her. Your bond. Welcome back, Tali. You had us worried for a while there. Without you, we began to crumble."

"Were falling apart? Like sandcastle when tide comes in?"

"My, how apt," Charles laughed, wiping his eyes. "Yes, like a ruined sandcastle. Kifo saved you when I could not. How do you feel?"

Tali ignored his question and released her grip on my shirt only to fling her arms around me and kiss me. It was an awkward, unskilled pressing of her lips against mine, but I gasped as she pulled back, feeling like our bond was somehow now complete and we really were one and the same being.

"Tali feels like is whole creature. Gave magic to Tali?"

"No magic, just our connection. Something changed, though."

"A joining," said Charles. "Breathing life into each other. You gave her your air, your life, and now she has returned the gift with one of her own."

"Was another gift?"

"Yes, I suppose it was." Our eyes met. Hers were that of a dragon once more, and I felt myself sink into them, lost to the vivid colors and the black pupil that I felt led directly into her head.

I see you, she said, as if reading my thoughts.

And I see you. You are hurting, but not telling us. You must tell us.

Is nothing. Will be better soon. Am immortal. Pain is nothing to dragon. Had pain before. Heal, and grow stronger than ever.

We need to get out of here.

Is good idea.

Oh no!

Is problem?

I'm not sure.

My eyes opened and I turned to a weary-looking Charles. His shoulders were slumped and his head hung low as if he didn't have the strength to remain standing much longer. I couldn't see what I was looking for, so asked, "Tell me you have it. Please tell me you have it."

"Have what? The will to carry on? Absolutely." He smiled weakly.

"No, he doesn't mean that," whispered Shi, realizing what I meant.

"Then what? You have me at a distinct disadvantage, I'm afraid," he said, shaking his head.

Tali stood, seemingly already recovering. As she loomed over us, body and hair dry, looking radiant, Bear clutched tight in her hand, she asked what we'd all been thinking.

"Where brooch?"

Charles frowned, then looked down at his closed fist. He opened his hand to reveal an empty palm.

"Shit," sighed Charles. Swearing, so I knew things were as bad as they seemed.

Shi batted at his father's shoulder and said, "Give me a few minutes, then I'll go look for the bloody brooch."

"Thank you. I will certainly join you, but I need to recover my breath. That was a close call. I thought we'd lost Tali for sure."

Shi turned his attention to Tali and asked, "Are you really okay? How do your lungs feel? They were full of water."

"Hurt, but am okay. But lungs not have water in. Cannot. Am dragon."

"Tali, you drowned," I tried to explain. "When that happens, our lungs fill with water so you can't breathe air. Then you die. We got the water out by blowing air into your lungs, forcing them to expel the water. Now you can breathe again, but it must hurt. I know it does."

"Am fine," she growled, genuinely cross. "Am dragon. Immortal. Not die in strange elf world. Not like. Want to go home. Will be dragon. No need be woman."

"No! You mustn't," I insisted. "Remember what we said. If you're in dragon form, the elves will sense you. You must remain a woman."

"Is hard. Am all wrong. Worried about if can shape-shift back."

I turned to Charles and asked, "How long could she do it for without being discovered?"

"No time. If she changes back, they will know, and then we will be discovered." He turned to Tali and asked, "Can you hold out a while longer? It's important. Our survival may depend on it."

Tali nodded, but clearly wasn't happy.

"What happened?" I asked Charles. "Why did we end up in the bloody lake?"

"Something must have moved the portal. I was very careful to picture the map and for us to land back from this small beach in the woods there. I felt the connection as the portal opened, and then as we stepped through something disrupted it. One moment we were about to emerge in the right place, the next it shifted and dumped us into the lake."

"And I think I know what it was," I sighed as I watched a small object bobbing about in the lake, slowly making its way towards us.

"I'll kill the stupid shit," growled Shi.

"You will do no such thing," said Charles. "I thought he was quiet when we left. He clearly decided to join us. Do not make him feel bad."

"Make him feel bad? He nearly killed all of us and look what happened to Tali. Who knows what damage he caused?"

"He just wanted to be involved," I said. "Don't make him get annoyed. Trust me, it's beyond hard work if he gets in a mood."

"Is Mai?" asked Tali as she turned to see what we were focused on. "Came too? Made portal move and drop us in lake?"

"I think he might have," said Charles. "But by accident, of course. Be nice, all of you."

Mai, a creature not of this world or ours, emerged from the lake with a smile on his face as he waved cheerily. He shook himself out and his hair resumed the static look, sticking out in all directions like his beard. His clothes were already dry. He smoothed down his housecoat, checked out the area with a bemused whistle, then ran excitedly up the beach on his short, stubby legs.

"My, that was rather unexpected," he beamed. "Hello everybody. Bet you didn't expect to see Mai here."

"We sure didn't," grumbled Shi. Charles cast him a warning glance.

"Why are you here?" I asked. "I thought you were watching things at home? You didn't say you wanted to come."

"I hadn't decided until this morning. It was after your story last night. It got me thinking about what an adventure it has been living in the human world, so I thought it would be nice to come along and experience another one. Isn't it beautiful? And the water is so warm. But, Charles, why did you drop us into the lake? Isn't that bad for dragons? Can they swim? And can you all swim? I'm an excellent swimmer, but it was very unexpected."

"Enough!" barked Shi. "You're rambling, and we aren't in the mood."

Mai took a shocked step back and looked at us. A frown slowly formed on his wrinkled brown face. "What's the matter? Aren't you pleased to see me?"

"I'm always pleased to see you," I said. "But you should have asked. We needed to adjust the portal to accommodate you. And it's dangerous. You were meant to stay out of danger."

"Yeah, because now we've got to worry about you if something goes wrong. Which it has," snapped Shi.

"Enough!" Charles warned him.

"Did Mai do something wrong? What happened?" When nobody spoke, he came and sat beside me and Tali with his legs out in front of him. He inspected Tali, then jumped onto her lap and put his head to her chest. He grunted, then hopped off and stood before us, head bowed.

"I discredit your faith in me. I besmirch our friendship. I sully myself and all gnomes. Please accept my resignation. I shall return home, pack my things, and leave you. I am shamed and will never forgive myself. Tali, I dishonored you the most. You may eat me if you wish. I deserve it. Go on, turn into a dragon and eat me. Gobble me up. I'm only small, but gnomes are tasty. Take your time. I deserve it."

"Am allowed?" asked Tali.

"No, of course not," I sighed. "Mai, cut the crap and stop using such big words. You know you aren't going anywhere. Not that any of us can."

"I truly deserve to be eaten. I put the entire party in jeopardy and will feel the shame until my dying breath. I broke the portal and you were plunged into the water like me. Dragons can't get wet, certainly not have their lungs filled with water. Can you even breathe fire?"

"Not know. Must stay woman."

"I'm sure once Tali's insides dry out everything will be fine," said Charles. I frowned as I caught his eye—both of us knew that was highly doubtful.

"Is one way to get fire inside burning again. Tali feels it has gone. Fire is out. Doused. Elf water kill fire. Must get new one. Must be soon. In minutes, or is too late. Once out for long, never comes back. Is rule."

"Is that right?" I asked Charles. "I never knew that."

"Yes, it is true. I told this to Tali many years ago. It is in the book."

"I've scoured every page of that book, and it does not say that."

"Then I must have learned it elsewhere. Or Tali merely felt it to be true. But she's right. Without a new fire to ignite what embers that may still remain, it will be gone forever. Or at least many years. She can't be without her fire."

"Not real dragon without fire."

"This just gets worse and worse," muttered Shi.

"And Mai is to blame. Let's go home, then we can get Tali a new fire and I will lock myself in my cupboard until I'm old and gray. It should only take a few thousand years."

"Stop being so ridiculous," I snapped, unable to stand it a moment longer.

"I'm not being ridiculous. But don't you talk to me like that. You aren't my boss. We're equals, and look at your clothes. Look at your clothes! Only Tali is clean. The rest of you have rips and sand everywhere. Sand! It never goes away. You find it for years after and it plays havoc with the washer."

"Guess someone got over their guilt pretty quick," chuckled Shi.

"Stop making things worse," ordered Charles.

"Charles lost the brooch when we fell into the water," I explained. "We need to get it right now. Everyone except Tali needs to go into the water and search for it. Including you, Nava."

"I'll do my best, but without Tali beside us I can't last long."

"Neither can any of us," I admitted. "Spread out along the beach, dive in, and search quickly then return to recover close by Tali's side. Mai, you seem to be the exception and don't need Tali's presence. Correct?"

"Yes, Mai is fine alone. I will search the longest and redeem myself. What a grave error Mai made. Oh, the shame." Without waiting, he hopped to his feet and ran into the water then was gone.

Reluctantly, leaving Tali on the beach, the rest of us waded into Lake Elinor.

Confusing Times

My eyes had acclimatized to the water now, but vision remained somewhat blurry. Nevertheless, I searched and searched, running my hands along the lake bed, sifting through the fine silt. The only problem being, it clouded the water, making it harder to see and causing more problems for us. To my left and right the others were doing the same, while Nava paddled around, checking if the brooch might be floating.

Soon, a wide swathe of the lake became murky, with silt glinting as the sun's rays refracted. I found nothing but pebbles. Within seconds, my heart began to hammer and my head grew fuzzy as pain crept into my bones as though the marrow was being gnawed. I lost track of what I was meant to be doing and took a deep breath, forgetting I was underwater. Coughing as I broke the surface, I splashed my way to the shallows, utterly uncoordinated.

Panicked, I scrambled to the shore and staggered out to find the others emerging, gasping for breath and mumbling incoherently. Shi's face was bright red, Charles was the opposite, looking like he'd seen a ghost. Maybe he had.

Tali eased forward cautiously, mindful of the water, seemingly unable to bring herself to even get her feet wet. Maybe she feared osmosis. Was it possible it even worked like that for her kind? Or was this my mind playing tricks on me?

The closer I got to her, the less pain I suffered and the easier thinking became until I collapsed by her side, gasping for air as my lungs burned. The others joined me soon after, and we lay there, already exhausted, with nothing to show for our efforts.

Nobody spoke, and minutes later we stood, nodded to one another, and tried again.

This time I swam out as far as I approximated we'd been when we arrived, then dove to the lake bed where the water remained relatively clear. I was in trouble almost instantly, unable to cope with the distance from Tali. The ringing in my ears became a thundering crescendo, unbearable as bodily functions began to shut down, once more preparing for death. Ignoring the growing pain and rising panic at being unable to breathe underwater, I searched and searched, more frantic and exasperated moment after terrifying moment.

I shoved off with my feet and sucked in air once I surfaced, then floated on my back and kicked with my feet until I made it to the shallows. Reluctantly, I flipped over, got my footing, and waded ashore before collapsing beside the others who had already returned.

"Anyone got it?" I asked, coughing, then purging the sweet water that had got into my lungs.

"Nope," spluttered Shi.

"Nava, you okay?"

"Can't go again for a while. I'm sick as a dog," he panted, grinning miserably.

"You rest up. It's taking more out of you because you're smaller. Where do we look now? Have we covered the area we swam from?"

"We need to check there," said Charles, pointing south-west. "There is a very subtle flow to the lake where it runs towards the populated area, so the brooch might have been carried that way."

"Okay, let's do this. I can't take it much more, but I guess we have no choice."

"Not if we want to get home," said Shi.

"How are you feeling?" I asked. "Apart from exhausted and hurting all over? Do you think the water has cured you?"

"Who knows?" he shrugged. "I'm not even sure I'm in one piece, to tell the truth. Damn, but it hurts being here."

"I know how you feel. But I think it's working. My nose has mended already. I'm a fast healer, but not that fast." I prodded my nose and there was no pain from the break. It just hurt as bad as the rest of me.

"We can check on our health once we find the brooch. We need to get it, and go now," said Charles. "We may have already drawn more attention to ourselves than is wanted."

"Meaning any?" I ventured.

"Exactly. The longer we remain, the more likely the elves are to come and investigate. Let's not give in. We are in no fit state for battle."

"We never give in," said Shi, getting to his feet awkwardly and heaving Charles up. He reached out and helped me up, and we headed back to the water.

I turned before I waded in and called out, "Stay safe, and ensure you don't stray far."

Tali will protect Nava.

Protect him, and protect yourself. I'm sorry about this. But we will return your fire, I promise.

With that, I readied myself, then plunged into Lake Elinor and let the pain become my world once more.

Charles and Shi were close by, so I followed their lead so the silt didn't interfere with their search and felt along the bottom, dredging with shaking hands, panic settling into my guts like a roiling molasses of potent poison. What if we didn't find it? What would happen? We'd be stuck, and captured by the elves. Killed, most likely, and innocents like Nava, Mai, and possibly even Tali would die because of our quest.

Maybe not innocent, but certainly not evil or cruel. All of us had killed, but for humans it was different. We made more choices, understood more about what we were doing, the effects of our actions. They were merely acting true to their natural instincts, never dealing with guilt or shame. Although, now I thought of it, maybe that wasn't true for Nava and Mai. Tali certainly never felt any guilt over acts of violence, but she did feel shame at times.

But Nava was a Necro creature, and smart with it. He didn't have human sensibilities, but he was a self-aware being, and maybe that always led to regret and cruelty. And as for Mai? I couldn't even begin to think about the strange house gnome's morality.

Something tugged my leg and in a panic I gulped water. With a kick, my leg was freed and I surfaced, retching badly as I swam towards the shore with a sickening sense of déjà vu. What the hell was in there? An elven Loch Ness monster that would devour intruders?

"What's wrong?" called Mai from right behind me.

"Did you just grab my leg?"

"Yes, it was Mai. Were you scared?" he asked, looking innocent, but I knew his game.

"You were trying to frighten me, weren't you?"

"Absolutely not. You should have more faith in your companions," he said, turning his face aside and chuckling quietly.

As I waded ashore, limbs feeling twice as heavy, sharp pain jabbing at my head and nerves, I suddenly realized I couldn't remember what I was just saying, and that I wasn't actually moving but was merely walking on the spot.

What was I doing? Why did I hurt so much?

I decided I was most likely dying, so slumped down and sat in the shallows, letting the agony wash over me and finally give me peace.

"Grab his other arm," came a voice from far, far away.

"Where is it?"

"Where's what?"

"His... er..."

Maybe I recognized the voices, but I wasn't sure, and it didn't matter anyway. Nothing mattered now because I was crumbling like a sandcastle. Had somebody said something about a sandcastle earlier? It seemed familiar. Should I build one? Was that why I was here?

Something hard slapped me across the face, jolting me back to this wet, unbearable reality.

My eyes must have been closed, because I opened them to find Mai standing on my legs, arm swinging at my face. He connected with a wet slap, the sting welcome.

"What was that for?" I grunted.

"You were probably going to die. Come, we must help Charles and Shi." Mai pointed at the two men beside me, both prone on their backs, the water lapping gently at their almost submerged faces.

"I don't think I can move. I can't feel my body. Do I still have my legs? Um, what are legs?"

"Your limbs are still intact. Mai will rescue everyone."

Suddenly, I was yanked from the water and was sliding backwards helplessly up the beach before being unceremoniously dumped.

Mai flashed down to the water's edge, and the next thing I knew, Charles and Shi were beside me, groaning as they coughed up water, and generally in as bad a state as me.

"Where... where's Tali? I don't feel better," I gasped.

Nava barked from behind us, so I turned my neck with darts of pain jabbing into my head, but I couldn't see him, or Tali.

"Something's wrong," croaked Charles, then stood awkwardly and stumbled up the shifting sand towards the woods.

"Help me up, please," I asked Mai.

Mai got behind me and shoved at my back, but it did nothing but push me down the beach. With a muffled scream, I rolled onto my side and somehow managed to get first onto my knees, then stand. I stumbled to Shi, hauled him up, and with the life draining from us we staggered after the retreating figure of Charles before he disappeared into the woods.

"Where's Tali?" asked Shi. "I can hardly move. Damn, this is the worst I've ever felt. We're going to die soon. I can feel it."

"She can't be gone. If she was, we'd already be dead. But we... What was I saying? Shi?" He was on the ground, convulsing, vomiting into the sparkling sand where it gave way to thick purplish grass that bent to avoid his purging.

Not quite knowing why, I nevertheless grabbed his arm and yanked him hard until he opened his eyes and the fit subsided. He screamed, a high-pitched animal wail that buoyed him into action, and he managed to stand. Hand in hand, we lurched forward, slowly coming back to ourselves as we entered the forest and brushed past smooth-barked trees then found ourselves in a clearing.

Smoke tickled my nostrils, causing me to sneeze, as I stared, aghast and confused, at a burning pyre. Flames licked at the stack of dry kindling and branches, climbing higher and higher. Tali stood in the middle of the fire, arms spread wide, a beatific smile on her arresting face.

We hurried forward. Her presence instantly cleared my head and I finally felt like myself again.

"What is she doing?" I asked Charles and Mai, who were moving closer and closer to the flames, heedless of the heat, drawn to her like moths to a flame.

"She's trying to get her fire ignited," said Charles.

"Tali is cold. She needs heat and flame to become whole again," said Mai like this was the most natural thing in the world.

"She'll be burned to a crisp," I cried, reaching forward to douse the flames. How, I had no idea, but I had to do something.

Charles grabbed my arm and said, "Stop! She is a dragon. She cannot be burned, or hurt. Maybe she can drown, but she can't catch fire. She's a shape-shifter, but her true nature is a dragon."

"Tali, what are you doing?" I called out, the flames licking around her belly.

"Tali getting fire back inside. Will add more wood? Lots of wood. Must burn Tali hot, then will have fire. Nearly lost, so must be quick. Do now?"

"Are you sure about this?" I called as the wood crackled and I took a step back.

"Am sure. Need big fire. Heat Tali inside, then can be dragon again. Without fire am stuck as woman. Must be large fire. Hot as inside volcano."

"She's stuck in that form?" I asked Charles.

"I'm not sure, as she hasn't tried to shift, but she might be right. It doesn't matter, as she needs the heat to ignite the flame. And without the brooch, we're going to need her protection as a dragon here if we want to survive."

"Mai has brooch," said the gnome as he held out his hand and revealed the precious elven silver. "It's why Mai tugged your leg in the water. Mai found it," he beamed.

"You did? That's great!" I whooped, scooping up the gnome and twirling him.

"Then let's give Tali what she wants and get out of here," chuckled Charles as he took the brooch from Mai and gripped it tight.

Nava ran forward with a log in his mouth, then dropped it into the fire before racing off to find more.

Snapping into action, cheering and joyous with the news we could go home, we set to work searching for dry wood. There was plenty about, fallen branches and old dead trees easy to find in the peaceful forest, so we piled more and more around the raging inferno until the flames licked high and Tali was engulfed.

We gathered around, the heat intense, and watched as Tali smiled from within the pyre.

"Is so nice and warm," she called out, joyous. "Tali feels like dragon again."

"How long do you need?" I shouted. "When will your fire be stoked again?"

"Not long. Need to be pure first."

"Pure?"

"I think I understand," said Charles with a nod to her changing form.

The clothes Tali wore were real in one sense, yet nothing but part of her camouflage ability in another, and slowly the gown she wore shimmered then became translucent before it was gone. Tali radiated astonishing beauty in her nakedness, her figure the personification of womanhood. Yet it wasn't her magnificent body that caused this feeling, but an inner purity that emanated as if she were the Mother Goddess from where all life originated.

She was undoubtedly beyond gorgeous, and I gasped as I was transfixed by her naked form, but it went deeper than that, latched onto something more primordial, more important. Tali lifted her arms out and laughed as she flung her head back and absorbed power from the flames, maybe from this peculiar land too, and filled until fit to bursting with a beatific magnificence. Her pale skin warmed, then took on an orange hue before she turned completely red and her hair darkened until it was as lustrous and bright as the flames.

Tali's eyes snapped open, glowing with an otherworldly intensity that left me gasping.

A smile spread across her innocent face as her form shimmered, and for a brief moment a glimpse of the dragon could be seen.

Slowly, the flames died down, then abruptly they were nothing but embers as Tali devoured the energy and drew it all into herself. Light shot from her mouth as she cried out in ecstasy. Her color faded, her hair and skin once more pale and golden, and then she was clothed, her flesh hidden. But I knew I could never forget it.

Does the fire burn again?

Stronger than ever, she gasped, emanating joy into my mind.

Wonderful! I felt her happiness, and it lifted my spirits, scouring away the pain of earlier, leaving me at peace. *I was worried about you. I was scared.*

Tali felt scared too, she admitted. *Dragon needs fire. Want to buuuuurn*, she hissed.

Maybe later, I laughed. *How about we get home first?*

Yes. Home. Shi is cured? And Nava's leg is better?

Let's check. Are you coming out of the fire?

Yes. Is done.

Tali stepped from the embers, retrieved Bear, and closed the short distance like she was gliding above the ground. Energy radiated from every pore, as though she truly had become more than she was previously.

"You look wonderful," said Charles, beaming at Tali.

"Feel best."

"And you're glowing," noted Shi.

"Mai is happy for Tali."

"Can we get out of here?" whined Nava.

"How are you doing?" I asked him. "Is the leg better?"

Nava shook out each leg in turn, then spun around, faster and faster, until a blur. When he stopped, he was smiling widely and panting with happiness. "I feel amazing! Like I'm twice the dog I was."

Tali placed Bear on the ground and hugged us each in turn. Everyone smiled, as though she'd shared her newfound power with us. Maybe she had.

"Shi, how you doing?" I asked.

"Same as the rest of you. Like I could smash a mountain or jump to the moon. I'm guessing the water worked, and I've been cured of the curse that has ruined my life."

"Everyone else good?" I asked.

"Mai could clean ten houses," laughed the gnome, then ran a fast circuit around the dying fire before returning and hopping up and down to burn off the excess energy.

"I'm feeling good too. Great, in fact. Full of life and power. The water really works. After what we've just been through, I expected my lungs to burn for days. But they're clear, seem like they're better than ever, same as everything else. Charles, how about you?"

"As though I could conquer the world," he admitted, but then he frowned. "I'm not sure we should feel quite this good. It's beyond curing any problems we might have had. It's as though its added to us somehow, made us more than we were."

"Then let's get out of here and back home," I said, resisting an urge to burst into song.

We wandered back to the beach, the disturbed sand all that remained of the danger we'd endured, the near-death we'd experienced.

Still confounded by what had happened, we sat for a while to recover our senses fully. Tali played with the sand, and made a rudimentary castle complete with a little moat. I smiled at her, pleased she still had such childlike actions within her.

Soon enough, Charles called us to action, so we spread out to our allotted positions with Mai close by my side. Charles opened his palm and held the brooch up so it caught the light from a sun I understood was not ours. It glinted as he pressed his thumb to the center and a pinprick of light popped into existence with an implosion of sound.

The portal opened, an eye back into our world and to home. I longed for the familiarity, for peace, and an end to this crazy time.

As the eye elongated to accommodate us, my heart soared with intense joy.

We were going home.

We'd actually done it.

Dubious Decisions

We whooped with delight as we stepped from the beach onto the compacted earth of the compound. My compound.

Home.

Birds sang in welcome. A gentle breeze whispered through the trees and caressed us as it passed. The tang of pine and disturbed earth filled my nostrils—usually so taken for granted, I could have wept for the joy it brought me.

Lights lit up the house and compound and the sensors flicked on as we staggered away from the portal.

"Is night?" asked Tali.

"Time can get somewhat disturbed when using such trinkets," said Charles, studying the brooch.

"Just shut the damn thing down and stomp on the bloody brooch," grumbled Shi as he turned to glower at the portal.

"That probably isn't wise," said Charles.

"Why not? We don't want to go back there, do we?"

"No, but you never know what the future holds."

"I do. A load of damn elves coming back to get their brooch. I'm surprised they held off this long."

"My guess is they are very rare and they can't get hold of another, or they've been instructed to lick their wounds and admit they were bested."

"That doesn't sound like something the elves would do," I noted.

"No, it doesn't," agreed Charles. "But let's close the portal."

We turned to look at the portal and the view it afforded of the beach and back into the woods. The fire could be seen glinting through the strange trees.

Mai and Nava dashed off to the house, Mai most likely needing to emergency dust, and Nava most likely to just get away from the craziness and curl up out of harm's way.

Charles lifted the brooch and smiled at us. As he pressed the central stone, Tali shrilled, "Bear is there," and without pausing, she dashed towards the portal.

Acting on instinct, I rushed after her as I called out, "No, wait!" but she passed over the boundary as I reached out to grab her hand. She turned, eyes wide with the understanding of what she'd just done, and I stumbled as one world shifted into another and fell flat on my face into the sand.

Rolling, I was on my feet in an instant and grabbed Tali's hand as we spun to get back to safety.

Charles and Shi were hollering from the other side, and waving frantically, clearly telling us to hurry as the portal contracted.

It blinked out of existence, leaving Tali and me stranded in the elven homeworld without any possible way to get home.

"Tali did bad thing," she said.

"It's not your fault. You wanted to get Bear. Come on, let's go and pick the little fella up."

"Are not cross?" she asked, looking deep into my eyes to read the truth behind my words.

"Tali, my strange companion, I am not cross with you. You are a dragon, and you finally have something that means something to you. What it symbolizes is important, and I understand that you wanted it and acted on instinct. You did nothing wrong."

"Kifo speaks truth," she said.

"Yes. Come on, let's get Bear."

Still holding hands, we walked up the beach then entered the woods. Smoke hung low, trapped by the trees, lowering visibility. We were shrouded in the acrid haze as a gust of warm air spun it around the clearing.

Tali bent, so I reluctantly released her hand and she picked up Bear then held it close to her heart.

"Is prize from Charles. Is gift and prize too. Tali is strong. Is important."

"Yes, it is. Keep Bear close and let's go back to the beach. Hopefully, Charles and Shi will be return for us any moment."

Tali clutched Bear as though the teddy was a living, breathing creature. It was astonishing how she'd grown attached to it instantly, having never shown the slightest interest in material goods of any kind. Nava sometimes liked to play with ropes and even the occasional soft toy I picked up, but it was purely from the instinct to kill or practice feats of strength and to test his jaws. I'd never for one moment considered that a dragon would want what amounted to a comforter. Such things had always been beyond her comprehension. Was she becoming more human because she could shape-shift? Maybe acting like a woman was letting some of the human show itself.

We stared out at the water, bodies close, her warmth palpable. The fires had most definitely been stoked; the heat radiated from her bare arms.

"Charles will be long?" she asked.

"I have no idea. Hopefully not. I don't like being exposed this way. Chances are, we gave away our position the moment we arrived, and if not then the, er, smoke will have alerted the elves. They might think nothing of it, but someone might come to investigate. Maybe we should move back into the woods a little, just in case."

"Tali did wrong thing again?"

"No, I didn't mean that. I wouldn't expect you to even consider the smoke from the fire. Tali, I know you don't think how I do, and that's a good thing. Plus, the fact you aren't scared of anything means you don't consider things that a human might. You aren't worried about enemies or getting killed, so you have an utterly different mindset than us."

"Tali will kill enemies. Can kill elves?" she asked, turning to me, looking hopeful.

"Best not to if you can help it. I doubt they'd take kindly to you killing one of their own. Especially in their homeworld. Come on, let's move back to the tree line and we can keep lookout from there."

With a nervous glance out to the lake, and a sense of emptiness closing in, feeling the weight of this world on my shoulders, and trying to push down the growing sense of unease and the possibility we were trapped here, I led Tali up the beach. We sat in the shade of the impossibly tall trees and let the silence descend.

A tea green full moon rose over the hazy pink clouds far away in the distance, and at that moment I felt very small and very isolated. Not lonely, as Tali was by my side, sitting patiently without a thought in her head, but I feared for our future and for those back in our world where we belonged.

The minutes passed as my sense of frustration increased. I had no watch, not that it mattered, as I doubted time was the same here. It was night back home, which it shouldn't have been, but I wasted no time trying to figure it out as how could I?

Judging by the movement of the sun, we had now been waiting for hours. Maybe it was seconds for the others, or maybe something had happened. The longer we waited, the more concerned I became, and my unease grew as Tali slept beside me, curled up with Bear like a child taking a nap after a busy day of play.

This was getting ridiculous. We couldn't just hang around here and hope Charles and Shi returned. It could be days, months, and what would we do in the meantime? But what was the alternative? Leave here and hope they found us? How? Maybe Charles could find us with the brooch. He just had to keep focused and picture where he wanted the portal to open. So if he returned and we weren't here, surely he'd be able to reach us?

As long as he did it within the twenty-four hours, of course.

The day wore on. I sipped water from the lake—there was little point worrying if it was safe or not after how much we'd already ingested. As we'd traveled light, ill-prepared for an extended stay, the only food any of us had brought was jerky. I pulled it from my pocket and we chewed the salty dried meat. It was better than I'd expected after how long it had spent in the water.

The sun lowered behind us, the moon rose high. A pale apple in a foreign sky far, far from home.

Stars blinked into existence one by one, and as I mapped their positions it became very evident that we most definitely were not on an earth-equivalent, somehow hidden behind a veil but still close to, or within, our homeworld. We were somewhere else entirely. Yes, all manner of supernatural realms were linked to ours, and I'd always assumed they were maybe in a different dimension to our own, but still in the same location. Now I had proof that wasn't the case at all. So how were we linked? Why were we linked? And why did I suddenly care?

It was the quiet. My mind was wandering, trying to figure things out and understand what I could in case we truly were marooned.

Startled from my reverie, I listened intently, heightened hearing picking up on the slightest sound. I heard the trees rustling on an almost imperceptible breeze, faint footsteps of tiny creatures deep in the forest, and there it was again! A splash out in the water. Most likely just a fish, but I crouched cautiously, mindful of not making too large a target, and let my Necrosenses come to the fore.

A sweet, aromatic tang tickled my nostrils, familiar and intoxicating. I pushed my vision to the maximum in the low light, the water a pale green glass sheet, washed out and gray now it was lit only by the mocking moon behind wispy cloud.

I definitely wasn't imagining this! A splash. Like an oar gently gliding through the water. I stood, needing to get a better view, and spied a silhouette of a boat far out in the lake. At least one man was standing confidently, and one or two others rowing, the paddles moving rhythmically.

We must leave, I told Tali urgently.

She stirred from her slumber and asked, *Are elves?*

You say, 'is elves.'

You do?

Um, no, sorry. You say 'is it elves?' Never mind, time to go. Someone's coming and they won't be our friend. Let's go into the woods. Can you see well?

Like is day, said Tali as she stretched out then sent a sense of confusion into my head.

Am still woman? Thought was dragon again.

I'm surprised too. I assumed you couldn't hold the form this long. How do you feel?

Bad now am awake. Was dreaming of being dragon curled up on beach with Kifo. Need dream. Is strange place. Makes Tali dream. But am not dragon. Hurt now. Must be dragon soon for while.

Hold out as long as you can. We need to move quietly through the trees, and that will be hard in your proper form.

Could fly.

Not if we can help it. No way will we be hiding then. The whole country will know we're here, even if it is night. They'll sense you, and they might have weapons that can shoot you down. Let's go.

We slipped into the forest silently, dusk turning to night instantly. My pupils dilated to allow in as much light as possible as we hurried deeper into the unfamiliar terrain, but I found the going tough and could only make out the shapes of things, no detail. Tali had no such concerns and could see as well as in the daytime, so I held her hand as she led me deeper and deeper into the woods.

The forest floor was littered with a deep mulch of pine-needle like leaves almost feathery to the touch. Our footsteps were silent as we drifted this way and that, not knowing how far the woods went, the maps having faded out the further from the lake they got.

Trees as wide as a house and as tall as skyscrapers mingled with spindly saplings. Violet flowers littered the sides of paths formed by whatever creatures lived here. We followed the trails, better to remain silent, constantly moving and heading west then skirting around to the east as the forest thinned.

Now and then we stopped, straining to hear if we were being pursued, but we heard nothing, and saw nothing but blurs of rat-sized creatures rushing through the thinning undergrowth.

After what must have been several hours, we emerged to find we faced a fantastical mountain. Something seemed familiar about it as I craned my neck to look up, and as the moon emerged from behind the cloud I gasped, realizing this was the place we'd come to rescue Charles.

He'd said he believed this was where we'd come, but wasn't sure. Now there was no doubt about it. We'd begun at the far end of the valley and must have walked the length of the lake through the woods, which explained the steep gradient as we skirted the water. Now we were at the base of the jagged cliffs that rose up and up. Palatial houses, ornate open verandas, and porches larger than the buildings themselves were dotted about the mountain on seemingly natural flat outcrops to afford incredible views along the valley and of the waterfalls too far away to hear.

We traversed the rough ground, deciding our best chance meant going up. If we could lose our pursuers, and I had no doubt we were being followed, this was probably the ideal place to do it. We didn't know the woods, we didn't know the terrain, and we sure as shit didn't know what else to do, so we decided to try to hide in the mountain and maybe we'd find a way out of this place or Charles would arrive.

It was a dubious plan at best, but I was at a loss. Were we walking into the mouth of the beast, or increasing our chances of survival? I knew Tali had to rest, to sleep, and would soon revert to dragon form, so we had to find somewhere safe and secure. Up seemed like it afforded more opportunities than the woods, where we were utterly isolated from anything that might help us make it through the night.

We found a set of simple steps carved precisely into the rock, so we took them slowly and made switchback after switchback, climbing into wonderland. We passed several porches with covered roofs, seemingly there just to admire the view, while others were attached to houses that had no perimeter, just balconies to stop you falling over the edge. Others were little more than platforms with marble floors. We crept past them all, taking first one path then another, always aiming higher as nothing seemed secure enough to hide out in.

Lights shone from the organic buildings, misshapen windows affording glimpses of ornate interiors whilst others were monastic in their simplicity. We caught hurried views of elves inside, reading, cooking, the sights confounding as it made them seem like real people. I also spied strange electronic devices, 3D holographic projections, and other futuristic things we could only dream of back home.

But mostly they seemed to relish the open air. The gazebos, patios, platforms, and long stretches of marble I could only think of as landing strips were where most of them clearly preferred spending their time. But there must have only been a few dozen properties, no doubt reserved for the richest, most powerful being so close to the lake, so we avoided any contact without issue.

We found ourselves on a narrow, jutting platform, affording a glimpse of what still awaited us. A fantastical structure sat atop the summit of the cliff, spilling down over jagged outcroppings like it had melted into the rock itself. Towers, spires, battlements with crenelations, it had it all, and the thing was vast. A true castle akin to the best we had, it still blended in perfectly with the cliff and improved rather than degraded the majesty of this place.

How are your legs? You haven't had much practice with steps.

Are aching and burn. Is normal?

Yes, that's what mine feel like. This was very steep and we've come a long way. Do your lungs feel okay?

Are same. Burn, but is nothing.

We need to get inside out of sight. There's a doorway up ahead. We should go in and see if we can find somewhere to hide. At least for tonight. Then we can reassess in the morning if nobody comes for us.

Will be out of time. Brooch not work. No portal.

Maybe, maybe not. Time is different here. It's either already past time for them to come, or they have hours left. I just don't know. Right now, we need to hide.

Tali not like hiding. Is better to fight and burn.

Usually, I'd agree. But you pick your fights, and you pick your time to fight. We don't know who we might be battling and we aren't ready. You need to sleep. You keep almost shifting. I see the dragon emerging. If we're deep inside the cliff, you can become a dragon. The rock should shield you from their senses.

Are sure? Would like to be Tali again.

I'm not sure, no, but there's no choice. At least this way we stand a chance. Let's go.

We eased up the last few treacherous steps, mindful of the fact we could tumble to our certain death if we fell, then ducked through the low doorway into we didn't know what.

Feel the Burn

We followed a spiral staircase, twisting around endlessly. Damp dripped from the central pillar supporting the steps, but we both gripped it as best we could, every step burning. The moist, still air hung heavy, making it hard to get enough into our lungs. Tali wheezed from just in front as I tried to stifle a cough caught in my throat that threatened to burst free at any moment.

How far does this go up?
Long way. Maybe hundred more steps.
Do you know how many a hundred is?
Is lots?
Yes, it is.

We were forced to use our hands on the steps above to help drag our weary bodies up, the cold seeping into my bones so I couldn't imagine how awful this was for Tali.

Just as I had the thought, an orange glow lit up the tower and I gasped as I realized it was Tali herself lighting our way.

Tali was too cold, she said, sending a shiver into my head. *Bring fire to skin. Is okay. Works.*

Yes, it works. It doesn't hurt? You aren't causing any damage?

No, is nice. Warm. Is magic maybe from witch Tali eat?

I guess. We knew you might be able to harness her more innate magic as well as take on her form. Seems you can. But keep the light low, and if you hear anyone, douse it immediately. We don't want to be discovered.

I received a mental nod as Tali ascended with renewed vigor.

Being in an enclosed space like this was torturous. For Tali, it would be much worse. Neither of us liked being indoors, and inside the mountain was akin to being buried alive.

Thankfully, after just a few dozen more steps, we came to a passageway that branched off from the stairs that continued upward.

Let's try in here. We might be able to rest and you can change into your beautiful dragon form.

Will be nice, sighed Tali, her voice sounding faint even when speaking silently.

We ducked into the low, curved passage. The ceiling was lined with brick, but the walls and floor were bare rock. It was even damper in here, and the air was stale. I worried we might catch some alien elf form of mold spore in our lungs that would proliferate and cause irrevocable damage, but then chuckled to myself as, currently, that was the least of our problems.

With my legs still burning, and now my back aching because we had to stoop, I trailed after Tali and the weak, stuttering light she cast on the sparkling rock. We'd hardly gone anywhere before more tunnels fed from either side. The strange language of the elves, carried on perfumed fresh air, echoed through the tunnels, and from others came divine smells that truly were out of this world. We hurried past, not wanting to risk discovery, then Tali paused at an opening, her head cocked to one side.

Think is empty. Not hear any funny elves. Should go?

I don't think we have a choice. At least the ceiling's higher so we can stand up, and we need to get somewhere safe. Somewhere large enough for you to shift. Let's try it.

Tali led again, and we followed the twisting tunnel that grew larger the farther in we went, but still not big enough for her dragon form. The bare rock floor changed to pale marble with veins of pink as the light levels increased.

We must be approaching outside, or maybe a house, so stay silent and keep to the walls. Don't be seen.

Need to rest. Must sleep soon.

I know. Hang in there. You're doing great.

Tali's pride rang into my head, but I sensed her exhaustion and moved beside her to encourage a final, hopefully brief, walk.

Hugging the now smooth wall, we approached the light and soon found ourselves in a large oval room with a high ceiling and a round window affording a glimpse of the night sky. The tea green moon peeked through the skylight as if to mock us.

More tunnels led off this strange room. I chose the one that was the darkest and led the way with Tali gripping my hand as she stumbled. It wasn't so much a tunnel as a doorway, and after several steps we emerged into a regular-sized room that left my head spinning and my senses reeling.

A man—no, an elf, I had to remind myself—was humming to himself as he chopped a carrot analog at what I supposed was a kitchen counter, although this was no kitchen I had ever seen before. It had a large table and eight chairs made from a beautiful blond oak or equivalent. Cupboards of the same wood lined one wall, with a peculiar hole that sparkled with silver and red where a conventional oven would usually be.

I stifled a gasp as Tali's fingernails dug into my palm, and the elf paused his humming as his shoulders tensed.

Shit.

With impressive speed, the tall, even by their standards, elf spun and flung the knife at us. Even in my current state, I managed to whip Ziggy up. His blade sank deep into the club and rang out as it vibrated.

"We don't want any trouble," I gasped.

"A human! A filthy human in my home! Two of you disgusting creatures. You stink." He backed away to a knife stand and pulled out a much longer blade as I grabbed the one stuck in Ziggy and pulled it free.

"That's not nice. We're sorry to intrude, truly we are, but can we rest here? If you keep quiet, I can, er..." What could I offer him as payment?

"Will be grateful," croaked Tali.

"Very," I agreed.

"You want to stay in my home? Stink out the place? Are you insane? I knew you humans smelled bad, everyone says you do, but I had no idea how foul. I'll kill you both and be famous. Yes, that's what I'll do," he said, smiling wickedly as he licked his lips and inspected the knife he held tight.

"There's no need for that. Wouldn't you rather be friends?" I grunted, sick of the bad attitude and utter hostility the elves had. Fair enough, we'd broken into his home, but still.

"Friends?" he laughed. "I watch you in the arena on the screen, see what you perverted Necros do to each other, and you think I would be friends with something like you? You are as mad as everyone says you are. Now die, you dirty maggots."

With a roar, he charged.

Elves may be slim, and lightly muscled, and smarmy as can be, but one thing they are decent at is fighting, as I soon discovered.

The homeowner was no fool, and as he approached he feinted left then jabbed out to the right with his knife, going for Tali who was groaning quietly. I blocked with Ziggy as Tali's eyes snapped to alertness and she punched the elf in the guts. He flew across the room and his head went straight into the black hole. He screamed as the machine beeped at him and a rush of heated air reached us. He pulled free and turned, face black.

"Now that is a hazard. Haven't you heard of safety first? What if you have kids? They'd cook themselves before breakfast."

"Stop talking. Your voice offends my ears," he growled as he charged again, this time grinning, clearly enjoying himself.

"Let's sort that issue out then," I hissed.

As the knife swished and I danced back to avoid getting my throat slit, I willed Ziggy into a slender fencing foil, the razor-sharp and very thin blade perfect for fast movement and light enough for my leaden limbs. It swished as I cut two fast lines in the air, the second successful at removing his ear cleanly.

The shocked elf sprang away to the other side of the table as he hissed in pain, but didn't scream. He put a hand to the wound as he stared at the ear on the floor.

"Better?" I asked. "Come here, and I'll remove the other one. That way, you won't have to be offended by my voice."

"What was that?" he asked, giggling like this was a game. "Do you get the joke?"

"Yeah," I grunted, "you're a real comedian." I launched onto the table, scattering chairs, and kicked up into his jaw, sending him slamming into the wall of cupboards. He bounced back and lunged with the knife, almost taking my legs from under me as he gripped my calf with his free hand and yanked. I booted him again, but awkwardly, and just got his shoulder. He grunted, then stabbed out.

I shook him free and narrowly avoided the blade, but slid on the polished wood and landed hard on my ass. He whooped with glee, then pounced on me. Either he knew something I didn't, or it was a plain foolish move made by someone who never fought outside of training practice, but either way, I just punched out with Ziggy—now a compact knife—and punctured his stomach.

"Damn, but you smell nice. It's enough to make a guy turn." I breathed in deeply, my head swimming with his wondrous scent.

"Never," he growled into my ear, then slid off, clutching his stomach as he crumpled to the obsidian floor.

"This guy was not very friendly," I noted to Tali as she moved to his side and looked down at him.

"You filthy humans. You desecrated my sacred space. No other is allowed inside such a private area. It is for me and me alone. How backwards you are. But at least I will have a tale to tell," he laughed as he got onto all fours then used the table to help him stand.

Tali punched at the base of his neck from behind and yanked out part of his spinal column.

"Let's go," I told her. "We can't stay here now. It's too risky."

"Can't just sleep here?" she yawned, watching without emotion as the elf twitched.

"No. He might have family, which is a shame, but even if he doesn't it might set off alarms somehow. For all I know, they have health trackers or who knows what. This place gives me the creeps anyway." I glared at the black hole in the cupboards suspiciously, like it might fry our brains. Could it?

I glanced out of the window and sighed. We were still too close to ground level, nowhere near as high up as I'd envisioned, and that wasn't good. We needed to be deep into the heart of the mountain if we were to stand a chance of making it to morning. We had no choice but to keep going for as long as we could.

I led a reluctant Tali out of the room and back the way we'd come. We ignored the other tunnels and retraced our steps right back to the stairs, then continued to climb.

Every step was torture, each footfall compounding the pain in my thighs and the general sense of unease I got in this spiraling catacomb. I'd expected to feel great after the healing powers of the lake, but seemingly that wasn't the case now. Yes, I was recovering quickly, but the terrible toll this world had on my body was too extreme for me to fully recover from. Every time Tali got a few steps ahead of me, it worsened, and I wondered if using the portal was also part of the problem. Like one giant morph that sapped all energy and left you more exposed to pain.

Can't go any further, Tali pleaded. *Am going to be dragon any minute. Must find safe place fast.*

Okay, there's light up ahead, so there must be another side tunnel. We'll go through and hopefully we can hide out. Be strong.

Am always strong. But is too long as woman. Must be Tali.

You will be. Here we are. Let's go through.

We peered into the darkness of another low tunnel, but it curved, blocking the view, so with no other choice, we headed into the unknown once more.

A Resting Place

We staggered along the tunnel, wheezing as we breathed in sour air before finally emerging through a small, open doorway and entered a huge cave that appeared to be a bloody impressive stable of some kind.

I stopped by Tali's side and sniffed the air, copying my beloved. Her sensitive tongue darted in and out, tasting the peculiar tang.

"Smells like dung and animal," she noted.

Speak into my head. We don't want them to hear us.

Animals already know are here. Can sense.

Let's move slowly. Stick to the far wall well away from them. Can you even see the end of this cavern? It's enormous.

Can. Is far. Are big creatures. Can feel minds. Not happy. Want say hello?

No, I do not.

The space was vast, and I figured it must run the entire length of the mountain. We'd emerged at the far end and there was no other way to get past as far as I could see. We kept to the shadows of the thankfully dry wall, an acrid taste on my tongue as I sucked in bone-dry air.

The rough-hewn floor of bare rock was great to grip and we hurried without making a sound. Across the empty space, as large as a football field of old, were endless stalls with gates twenty feet tall supported by thick metal columns that reached up to the curved ceiling. What the hell did they keep in here?

At approximately the halfway point, I made out a pinprick of light at the far end, so we redoubled our efforts and made good time. Grunts and snores echoed off the walls, chains rattled, the doors banged, the huge locks clearly being tested as unseen creatures slammed against them in their sleep.

At the far side, we paused to get our breath back and I approximated at least fifty of the massive enclosures. At least half were locked. Were they occupied? The smell was more intense here, so maybe this was where most were kept. It didn't matter. We were out of it now, and we eased forward through an opening larger than a house onto a wide platform jutting out into nothingness.

Intrigued, and with nobody around, we followed the platform right to the end. It took minutes. The ground was the same rough stone, tool marks still visible, and so different to the rest of the architecture. What was also very apparent was the lack of any form of railing. I assumed the animals launched and came in to land here. Were they dragons, or an elven equivalent?

We stepped away from the wall and peered down into the beautiful valley far below.

Tali dropped to the ground, sat on the edge, and swung her legs.

Is nice. Should sit.

It's bloody terrifying is what is.

Why? Is just high. Won't fall. Why would you?

I know I won't fall, but tell my brain that. It's a basic human instinct to be afraid of heights. We die if we fall, so it's best to stay away.

Still scared even after flying with Tali so long? she asked, intrigued.

Yes. It's terrifying every single time.
Kifo is silly man.
You can bet your life on it I am, I chuckled silently.

Nevertheless, fighting every instinct to run back into the cavern and play with the beasts, I sat, then shuffled forward until my legs dangled in the air.

"Did you ever think we'd be sitting at the top of a mountain in the elven homeworld?" I laughed.

"Tali thought would do everything. Is limits?"

"There are limits, at least for humans. I guess you have a different outlook on life."

"Because am immortal. Or thought was. Died in water?"

"Yes, you did. Because you had human lungs, I suppose. Or maybe dragons can drown, although I don't believe so. Hey, maybe we just thought you were dead. Maybe something would have happened and you'd have reverted to a dragon after a while and been fine. It was scary though. I didn't want to lose you."

"Not want to be lost. Will see everything. Kifo will be there?"

I turned to Tali, and told her the truth. "No, not always. For a long time, yes, but not forever. You will live so long, it's hard to imagine such a thing. I won't. Something will happen and I'll die. Either fighting, or just bad luck, or old age. Even Necros die. It will be hundreds and hundreds, maybe even a thousand years or more if I'm very lucky, but it will happen."

"Tali will be alone then," she said softly. "Not want that. Want you."

"I know, but you have to just enjoy the time we have. Nothing lasts forever. Not even immortal dragons. One day, you will be very different to how you are now. You will be a wise old dragon living somewhere far away in a strange land with other ancient dragons for company. But there will be so many memories, so many centuries of them, that you won't recall most. Everything will fade and you will be a different creature."

Will always remember this time, Tali said into my head, radiating happiness. She shuffled closer, the intense heat of her body so comforting.

So will I. Forever. Just you and me atop a mountain.

We sat in silence, listening to the distant tumbling of the waterfalls, the muted calls of animals far below, and the cry of birds hunting in the valley. The air was scented with flowers I would never know the names of, but the sweetness lent itself to the intensity of the time we spent together. The balmy air was perfect, the moon at its zenith now, casting everything in an otherworldly green light that brought home how far away from our old life we'd come.

"Come on, it's time to go hide. We shouldn't be here. It's dangerous and silly. Charles isn't coming, at least not tonight. We need to hide until morning, then go back to the beach. Maybe he'll be there waiting for us."

"And elves wait too. Were on boat."

"That's a chance we'll have to take. You need to become a dragon, so let's go back into the cavern and get to the opposite end, then you can change. The doors to the stalls were open, so they shouldn't sense us that far away."

"Is good idea. Feel like will burst from skin. Not enjoy this place. Like it here, with you, but hate elves," she added.

"I like it here with you, too." I stood, then reached out my hand and helped Tali to her feet. With the large moon behind us, we embraced, a man and a dragon on a fantastical mountain with a kingdom of strange beings all around us. We held each other, never wanting to let go, knowing we had to.

With a sigh, I released Tali and we moved swiftly back into the cavern and rushed to the far end as she began to stumble and her form shifted to that of a dragon.

By the time we made it, she was almost doubled over, the effort finally too much for her. She slumped to the ground and became her true self once more.

After spending so much time with her as a woman, it took my breath away to see her in all her majesty. She was so large, so perfect, and so deadly looking that I was amazed.

"Sleep well, and tomorrow we will find a way out of here."

Tali clutched Bear tight and curled up, resting her head on her tail, then was asleep.

"Wake up. Tali, we have to go!" I hissed.

Tali opened a lazy eye and yawned, intense sulfur and heat singing my facial hair. The fires were definitely burning strong again.

"Is problem?"

"Yes, there's someone at the far end. We have to go. Come on."

Tali lumbered to her feet and stretched out, her wings creaking like old leather. She hadn't flown for a while and the stiffness showed as she stumbled.

"Feel wrong. Body not work properly."

"I know. You were in human form too long. You need to fly. But not now. Become the woman again, and quick." I glanced ahead but couldn't see a thing from so far away. But we weren't alone, the shouts of voices and the banging in the stalls all the information I needed.

Tali stilled, then shape-shifted into her alter-ego and we ran the short distance to the staircase and began to head down. We got only a few steps before we stopped when voices echoed up the tower.

Elves.

Back. We need to go back. There are at least three coming up and we can't fight in a confined space. Turn around.

It was tricky in such a narrow gap, but we turned then dashed back up and out into the cavern. I checked Ziggy was good to go, shunted my will into the magical club, then pulled him free as he became a sword. We raced past the stalls, staying close to the wall as we approached the closed ones, as I frantically searched for a different exit now there was some light. Where was it coming from? I glanced up to discover numerous openings far above letting the dawn light stream into this peculiar place.

But there was no other way out, nothing to do but keep on running, staying in the shadows and hoping we weren't seen. The voices from the stairs rang out loud and clear, but they were merely talking without being mindful of who heard, not shouting a warning, so we were still undiscovered.

We slowed, creeping forward, and I wondered if we should hide in a stall. But then we'd be trapped, and a fight out in the open always leaves you with more possibilities. We eased along the wall, mindful of the gap closing between us and those most likely searching for us, and whatever was up ahead.

We had to risk it, so we remained in the shadows and picked up the pace but didn't run for fear of being spotted. Nearly at the entrance, we stopped dead in our tracks as a woman called out.

"I don't care what you say. I think he's ready, and that should be enough for you."

"If you wish," said an elf in stable livery with his head bowed.

"So insolent!" she tutted, then bent and retrieved a tiny creature from the floor.

"Is dragon," gasped Tali.

"Yes, but be quiet," I whispered.

We watched as she placed the tiny wyrmling no bigger than a cat onto her shoulder. It nuzzled her ear as though talking to her, its long tail curled around her neck. The elf laughed, then turned her attention back to the male.

I looked past her to study a squad of guards standing to attention at the entrance, stiff and formal in ceremonial garb that was also very practical. Each had a shortsword at their side, chainmail, and an ornate helmet.

Focusing on the female, I caught the end of the conversation.

"...him now. It's time. Early morning is best. He is at his most energetic."

The stable master nodded, then walked over to the nearest stall and unlocked it. He flung the double doors wide, the planks as thick as my legs, to reveal an animal curled up asleep.

Behind us, the voices were getting closer, and the two elves paused and peered our way.

"Shit," I moaned, knowing we were screwed. *Keep back against the wall. We might get lucky.*

The female stared down the wide corridor at the approaching elves, then called out, "Who goes there?"

The guards drew their weapons.

"It's me, Eleron. We know they're here somewhere, at least some of them, and we got a scent of them coming this way."

"Indeed. And yet here you are, skulking around my castle at an ungodly hour without permission and upsetting my darlings."

"I apologize. But they are here."

Eleron and his two accomplices sped up so as not to offend this clearly important elf; she waited impatiently for them to approach. Then she spied us and I knew we had to act quickly.

Her eyes widened in surprise, then she smiled before ignoring us. What was that about? She didn't call out a warning, or look at us again, so it bought us a few seconds.

Tali, become the dragon and get us out of here. Right now.

Tali shape-shifted instantly into her dragon form. Pressed up against the wall as she was, dust rained down as her mighty form appeared. She bounded out into the open, so I ran after her, leaped up onto her back, and gripped the pommel as her wings spread wide and she flapped them to awaken the powerful muscles.

Elves shouted in warning from behind, the guards rushed forward and surrounded the regal female, and the stable master unlocked a collar around the complaining beast's neck fixed to a chain bolted to the ground. He urged the creature to wake up. Its eyes snapped open and as Tali thundered past, I caught sight of a saddle strapped to the beast's back, but had no time to take in its size or what it was as it was still curled up. All I knew was it had a lot of teeth, very large wings, and a tail longer than Tali's.

The guards ushered the elf woman aside as Tali took to the air, talons scraping the ground as we sped out of the cavern then across the platform before launching off the edge.

We were flying! Soaring into the valley as Tali beat her wings languidly, forcing the blood to pump and gradually build up to full strength.

The power beneath me was incredible. The sheer density of muscle and might left me breathless as it had so many times before, but this time it felt different. More intense, our connection deeper. Could a mere day here have changed her, or was it simply that my emotions and senses were so heightened with the adrenaline rushing through my veins?

We banked hard and Tali flapped her wings faster as we rose higher until I was looking down on the entire vista. The castle truly was huge, but I focused on the large outcrop and watched as groups of elves appeared. There was that female again, the guards surrounding her, staring up at us. For a moment, our eyes met, and I saw nothing but excitement reflected back at me. Then the strange beast from the cavern emerged and she shouted something to the rider, her face stern, but he called back, shaking his head, as the animal thundered along the platform then launched as we soared higher and Tali turned once again, heading into the valley.

For the first time, I got a proper look at what had been manacled inside.

A thick neck, but not long like Tali's, held a boxy head with deep-set eyes, slits for nostrils, no visible ears, and a wide, grinning mouth full of row after row of angled teeth. If it got hold of its prey, they would never get free before being torn to shreds.

Oversized wings were well-muscled and leathery, but with more bones than Tali's. The body itself was wide with a protruding belly and a fat, long tail that meant it would be extremely dexterous at making sharp turns when flying. The entire torso was smooth, a thick hide of dull gray with no markings whatsoever.

The rider sat astride a massive saddle but then shifted position to stand in the short stirrups, holding tight to a chunky leather rein he used to control the beast.

They were coming straight for us. As they approached, the beast tucked in its wings a little, its speed increasing as the rider tugged on the reins and it banked, the teeth of the creature exposed as it aimed for Tali's belly.

Aerial Acrobatics

Tali flipped her wings, literally putting the brakes on mid-air, and I gripped tight for fear of launching over her head and plummeting to my death.

The extraterrestrial teeth monster—I named it a ceph because the head was the bit that worried me—shot past, jaws snapping at air as Tali swept low then curved back up so fast I almost lost my seat.

We arrowed for the ceph and rider, who was searching for us, and Tali nipped at the creature's flank as we careened into the creature fast enough to cause whiplash. My beautiful dragon, in full bloodlust mode now, raked at the thick hide as we glided past the tumbling pair, a victory cry piercing the frigid air.

I gasped, finding it hard to catch my breath up here where the air was thinner, before holding on for dear life as Tali twisted, then tucked in her wings and we plummeted towards the bucking ceph and screaming rider.

A buzz of small silver drones tore across the sky then split into small groups and followed our every move. Were other elves watching on strange devices from the comfort of their homes, or large arenas where they munched on popcorn?

Thighs already burning from gripping the saddle, I grabbed the pommel tight with one hand and freed Ziggy with the other, hoping this fight would be over before it truly began. As we caught up with them, I let my weapon lengthen and stabbed out with the spear while Tali raked her talons across the back of the beast and tried to dislodge the rider.

He angled aside, Tali's momentum carrying us past too fast for me to get anything but an ineffective prod at the creature's hide. But it was enough for me to realize the animal could be hurt, as green blood oozed from the small wound and it shrieked into the void, smashing a glistening drone aside in anger with its thick tail.

It isn't immortal like you. It bleeds. We can kill it. I don't want to, as they must have an awful life chained up, but it won't stop until it destroys us, so let's finish this.

Tali will get rider. Without elf, teeth thing will not fight.

Good idea. They're more susceptible from above, so get high then go in for the kill.

With her wings flapping hard, Tali careened along the valley then performed a sickening loop-the-loop fast enough to pin me into the saddle. We were coming down headfirst at the ceph and rider, drones swarming around us all, so I adjusted Ziggy, holding the shaft tight under my arm, the point aiming straight at the man.

The rider glanced down then around, searching for us, but we were already upon him and I thrust Ziggy out as Tali snapped, intending to take his head clean off. But the ceph became aware of us at the last moment, and flipped sideways, causing me to get a hit on its tail; Tali missed altogether.

But they were spiraling badly, the incredible weight of this flying combatant too much for it to right itself quickly. Tali took instant advantage, having a much better distribution of weight, and by the seems of it much more experience in the air. As the peculiar xenomorph and frantic rider slowed their spin, Tali angled her wings so we came at them head-on, her front quarters extended, talons more than capable of ripping through the tough hide of the ceph and utterly shredding the rider.

Before it had the chance to stop its fall, we slammed into the head of the monster. Green blood burst from its blunt snout as it snapped at Tali, trying to tear away her eyes. I jabbed out, one, two, and punctured the neck several times as Tali clawed at the pale spots on its thick, writhing neck.

The rider hacked at Tali's limbs with a longsword, but it was futile as she was as resistant to attack as the mountain we had launched from, and he grunted as pain reverberated up his arm. I clubbed him with Ziggy in default mode and then we were past, chased by the voyeuristic cameras. I spun to watch, just like the drones, expecting to see him falling to his death, but he was slumped sideways in his saddle. It was then I noticed that he'd managed to strap himself on with thick leather belts, giving him much more freedom than I had on Tali. I needed such a device if aerial battles were a part of my future. I prayed they weren't.

Again, Tali dove and we raked past, her snapping at the ceph's head, me clubbing the rider, but neither were direct enough to put an end to this. The elf persevered with his sword attack, but Tali shrugged it off with an amused grunt as we sped across the valley before she arced much more gradually, giving her wings the chance to catch the thermals.

It gave me a few precious seconds to study our opponent. The rider was a lean, relatively stout elf by their standards, but lithe and very agile in the saddle—he was clearly a proficient rider and knew hand-to-hand aerial combat well. I did not. Maybe this was a sport akin to jousting? Was that what the animals were for? Bred to be champions? It made sense.

He wore lightweight chainmail and leather, so my guess was that today must have been a day dedicated to such sport unless it was his regular garb. The creature itself was fast, and very heavy with wings as large as Tali's, but the body wasn't as streamlined. It seemed rather a poor choice for combat like this, but there was no denying the power the thick jaws had, nor the ferocity of its attack. What it lacked were talons like Tali's, and the limbs were very short, but that signaled many generations of breeding to make it better in the air yet undoubtedly ineffective on the ground.

But what I focused on above all else were its eyes. They were sunk way too deep for it to have good peripheral vision, and that had been obvious during our attacks. It relied on the rider to direct it and give commands, and he spoke in the elven tongue to the beast so it was clearly smart enough to understand.

We needed to focus on its blind spots, and that way we would best this monster-headed enemy, although it pained me to destroy an animal clearly just doing what it had been trained to do. What other choice was there? They obviously used these animals for sick sport, and yet I knew we had to be ruthless to get out of this alive.

Tali beat her wings fast and hard, our speed astonishing as we raced against a sour wind, the stink of the beast reaching us on a sharp breeze.

Get behind it, then burn them. The wind's coming right at us, so if we face the other way the flames will carry further.

Joy rang in my head as Tali hissed, *Will buuuurn.*

With a slight adjustment to her approach, Tali pulled in her wings, lowered her head as if to attack, then swooped low suddenly and arced around behind our prey, even outmaneuvering the whining drones that so far weren't causing her any discomfort. Maybe elven technology didn't interfere with her faculties like ours did? With a swift arc, we sped towards our prey as the animal cried in frustration and began its own more cumbersome turn.

With the wind at my back, I hunkered low into the slipstream behind Tali's sinewy neck. The saddle warmed uncomfortably as the fires within my precious Tali screamed for release. My thighs felt ready to burst into flames as the intensity became almost too much. We were upon them. The rider turned to face me, sword held aloft to hack out; the ceph's neck arched as its body tried to whip around.

For a fleeting moment, the ceph was almost stationary as it completed its turn and Tali, instincts honed by years of hunting and countless assassination expeditions, straightened her neck, lowered her head, and opened her jaws wide. I vibrated in the saddle as her insides rumbled, then a fierce torrent of incredible heat shot from her gaping maw with such force that we were shunted backwards until she compensated by beating her wings.

Tali sprayed a vivid, extended burst of orange fire along the flank of the ceph from tail to head, catching the screaming, panicked rider as we passed close enough for me to slam Ziggy into his head, knocking him sideways in the saddle, but he couldn't avoid the destructive force of Tali's fire and was caught alight instantly. Several drones tumbled, clearly not built to withstand such extremes of heat.

As the ceph roared in pain, I thrust out with Ziggy in spear form and popped one of its black, beady eyes before we were past and the fire thankfully died.

Not finished, knowing it was never over until her enemy was slain, Tali flew up and around then came in for a second pass. This time slower, taking advantage of the disorientation caused. We approached from the right, Tali aware that the creature was unable to track us. The elf had righted in the saddle, his hair smoldering, face a vivid mess of blisters, but skin already beginning to heal. It didn't matter.

We knew we had won, and this was merely the coup de grâce.

With languid self-confidence, Tali sucked in elven air, her body vibrating again as she stoked the strange furnace within, then hissed before she expunged a tight ball of white-hot fire that blasted into the ceph's head, tearing half the jaw away. Its scream died mid-cry.

Brain irreparably damaged, the animal's wings beat frantically for a moment as we sailed past, then as we turned and Tali held her position riding the sweeter-smelling thermals above the burning rider and ceph, we watched it spasm before its head hung low to its belly on a limp neck and it dropped, dead, into the valley below. Drones gave morbid chase.

With the bloodlust still upon her, Tali dove, tearing after her already defeated foe, but still in control enough to know that if there was the slightest chance of it somehow regenerating what was lost this might not be over. I watched, amazed, as the head did begin to reform, but the rocky mountain was fast-approaching, and time was not on our enemy's side.

Tali hovered, just like the drones, as the ceph caught a jagged outcropping and smashed into the rock before thumping into the unforgiving cliff face over and over as it crashed to its death. The rider was thrown from the saddle, caught by a bootstrap as he was dashed repeatedly against the rocks until, finally, his leg was amputated at the knee and he was caught in a crevice. He might be an elf, and maybe he would eventually recover somehow, although I didn't see how, but we didn't have to worry about him anytime soon.

The ceph continued to tumble, a ball of bloody hide as it bounced from a smooth ledge, sailed out into the air, then slammed onto a vicious, spiked protrusion and was pierced right through its torso. It hung limp, belly exposed, rock protruding, and the body was finally still.

Tali drifted away from the victory scene with a cry of joy into the valley. She turned her sinuous neck and our eyes locked. Her red orbs slowly became the beautiful eyes I had stared into countless times over the years, and we smiled as the bloodlust faded and she carried us away from the battle scene.

The silver drones spun around us excitedly.

But then she turned, and she passed back over the lower reaches of the mountain, neck arching to inspect the kill.

They're dead. We won.

Tali want to check. Are elf and strange creature. Not know if come alive again.

They won't be returning from that any time soon. If elves are immortal, then that guy is going to have a long road to recovery.

Was good fight, Tali grunted. *But was not right.*

I know what you mean. They bred that poor thing to fight. It didn't have a choice. It was under the mental control of the rider. It was forced to act that way.

Not how should be. No... what is word?

No free will. It couldn't make its own decisions. It was forced into it.

Is bad. Not like elves.

I'm with you on that one, I chuckled, beyond relieved the battle was over. I was shaking badly and my head pounded—the aerial acrobatics had left my stomach in knots and every muscle ached from being so tense.

Let's land. We need to rest. You did so well. I'm very proud of you.

Tali nodded. *Am invincible. Best at fighting.*

You sure are, I agreed, stifling my mirth at her unquenchable self-confidence.

Tali beat her wings languidly as she circled above the mountain, then we sailed down and past the ledge where the woman of earlier was standing surrounded by her guards. As the drones circled her, she lifted a hand to shield her eyes from the sun, and I swear she nodded then smiled at us before she turned to say something to the wyrmling hopping around her shoulders excitedly.

I saluted, then focused ahead as Tali glided into the valley. We sped across the lake, Tali's talons disturbing the tranquil water, and then she turned and slowed before coming to land on the beach where we'd first arrived.

With trembling legs, and my head spinning, I slid from the saddle and sank gratefully to the coarse sand. I wobbled for several seconds, then leaned against Tali for support, before just collapsing to the ground.

"Kifo is unwell?" she asked, turning her neck to inspect me.

"I'm fine. Just a bit shaken from your expert flying."

"Was good?"

"Very. But it's a lot for any human body to cope with. We're meant to be the right way up. I think all the blood's pooled in my stomach or something. I feel sick."

"Are funny," laughed Tali, then collapsed suddenly, forcing me to jump aside before getting squashed.

"Tali! Are you okay?" I asked, my own dizziness forgotten.

"Legs weak. Am tired. Is hard to turn in air so much. Use much energy. And fire use more. Need food to build up muscles, be strong again."

"I know, and I'm sorry. I don't know what there is here to hunt, or even if you can eat it."

"Can eat any meat," she shrugged, then her body sagged even more and her tail thudded into the sand followed by her neck slumping before it too thumped into the ground, sending sand flying.

"I'm not so sure. And I haven't seen anything apart from the small creatures last night in the woods. We need to be careful, anyway. We don't know what's intelligent. We don't want to kill something that could be smart. Damn, where is Charles? We need to get out of this place, and we need to do it soon."

"Would like to go home," she admitted, voice fading as exhaustion took her over.

"Me too. More than anything. We need to leave here, though. They'll be coming for us. They already tracked us here once, but they will have watched us land this time. Those bloody drones see everything. A quick break, then we'll go. Tali?"

I got to my feet and walked around the rumbling dragon to find her eyes closed. She was asleep. Tali needed food to recover from such an impressive battle. But she would have to make do with a short rest then we needed to go. A few minutes at most was all I dared to allow, so with that in mind, I sat beside her head and cradled her snout. Her power was like a drug. Her might sank into me like I could absorb her essence as I took deep breaths through my nose and inhaled her intoxicating scent of sulfur, her very dragonness. How I loved her. How I feared for her in this peculiar place.

I placed Bear next to her nose, knowing it would please her to see it when she woke.

Fighting exhaustion, aware I dared not sleep, I set my mind to devising a plan. What should we do? Where should we go? Was anywhere safe in this world? Where even were we? A small island? A huge continent? At the heart of the elven kingdom, or in some backwater where nobody cared about its fate? I knew so little and it was irksome. I needed information, but had no way of getting any besides riding Tali and scouting out the area in detail. But we couldn't stray far from this locale, as if Charles returned the best place to be was here. Surely he'd check here first before trying to find us? Could he home in on my location or not?

So many questions.
I had answers for none of them.

Feeling Frisky

The minutes passed rapidly as my breathing slowed and a sense of serenity overcame my adrenaline. Rather than a major come-down, I was ready for anything. Was this the power of the water? Could Lake Elinor restore lost energy as well as mend wounds and cure injury? Or was this the world itself?

Tali stirred, then yawned as her eyes opened. I stood and smiled as she lifted her muzzle from the sand.

"How are you feeling?"

"Good. Like had big sleep and ate lots. But not right. Shouldn't feel this way." Tali got to her feet cautiously, then shook out her tail and cricked her neck before arching her back and peering down at me.

"You look so majestic. So proud and fierce and special."

"Kifo is special too."

"Thank you, but not like you. Do you think you're ready to leave?"

"Must be woman?"

"Yes, to at least try to hide your dragon essence. It's probably pointless, but we should at least attempt to hide our tracks. Plus, you won't fit between the trees otherwise."

Tali stared into the strange forest and snorted loudly. The heat forced me back, but I laughed for the sheer joy of being together.

Without another word, Tali shape-shifted gracefully into her human form. But she was naked, and almost burning up, as she reached out and touched my face gently then ran her shaking fingers across my chest. My heartbeat increased worryingly fast, and I flushed as I stammered, "What are you doing?"

"Have strange feeling inside. Can mate now?"

"We mustn't. It's bad timing, and I'm not sure either of us are ready for that. We are in a strange world with people chasing us who want us dead, and this is just the adrenaline after the fight. It makes you, er, horny."

"Tali has horns?" she reached up to her head, then frowned and said, "Not there."

"It means something else. When you want to mate. Tali, you are new to your human form and don't understand everything that goes on inside it. It's just hormones rushing through your system. The excitement of the fight. It stirs things inside."

"Not want to mate?" she asked, stepping close, her perfect figure overwhelming my senses as I breathed in her musk and felt myself succumbing. Was this right? Or very wrong? How many times would I ask myself this?

"I love you, and yes, I do, but we mustn't rush this. It might be a very bad idea. You have no experience, and don't even understand your anatomy. And you are young. I'm not sure if this breaks rules or not."

"Am adult. Like Kifo. Know about sex and how works. Have urges when dragon same as when woman. Feel different but same."

"That's, er, good to know." I glanced down at her naked flesh and reached out, then snapped my arm back to my side and said, "We'll talk about this at home. We need all the energy we have, and we need to remain vigilant. Understand? This is too important to rush. I will not risk our bond. We must be sure."

"Tali is sure. Am animal and know is right. But yes, am human, and hand feels different, body too. Not understand all. Go home, then use bed."

"I think Mai will have a thing or two to say about that," I chuckled.

"Miss Mai. Want to see."

"Me too. So very much."

With a nod, Tali let her gown cover her skin and I rubbed at my face, sighing with relief. Were Charles and Shi correct, and this was inevitable? Was it fair on her or me? Deep down inside I felt this was right, that we were destined to be together, but what if I was wrong? And how could this possibly work? Then I realized that ever since we were bathed in each other's blood we had been together more than apart.

Maybe this was what I'd been searching for my whole life. The missing piece of a puzzle I didn't even know was incomplete.

Or, and I shuddered, it would be the downfall of all I held dear in this life. Was it worth the risk?

Necrosenses snapped into heightened action as I felt a rend in the fabric of this eerie world. Not a portal, but the almost imperceptible prelude to someone, or some thing's, morph.

Ziggy was only halfway from his holster, and Tali was still in human form, but the air was displaced as the woman we'd seen earlier arrived several paces up the beach, looking calm, composed, and without any after-effects from her morph. Her wyrmling draped its tail down her chest and peered at us with eyes as inquisitive as those of its mistress.

She wore a simple dress of emerald green with gold braid and fine embroidery, a pendant in the same style as the brooch we'd taken hung over the figure-hugging silk with a tight collar, and she was barefoot. Her eyes were the usual pale blue of the elves, but unlike any others I'd seen, hers were genuinely warm and danced with mirth. With fine-boned features, and delicious pointed ears, she was the epitome of a friendly elf. But I knew different. I'd seen her barking orders at the man who tried to kill us, and it was clear she was responsible for the incarceration of the cephs.

"Doesn't the human speak?" she chuckled. The wyrmling whispered something into her ear and she laughed, hearty and loud.

"My little friend wishes to know if Tali truly is a dragon?"

"You know her name?" I asked, casting a warning glance to Tali, who bristled at the insult.

"I know all about you, Kifo."

"And you are?"

"Names are powerful. You will know mine in time, just not now."

"You control those animals? You shackle them and force them to fight?"

"Some of my kind are stuck in their ways. I apologize. If my opinions were heeded, there would be no slavery. Yes, they are trained and bred to fight, but they still need riders to control them. Poor things."

"And you own them?"

"In a manner of speaking, but not really. Our life here is complicated, as I'm sure you can already tell. Things are not always as they seem."

"Then what's your role in all this? Have you come to kill us?"

"Just the opposite. To save you. From one bonded soul to another. My dear wyrmling is my world, and such a rare and beautiful creature. Now I get to meet another dragon." The elf walked forward cautiously, careful not to make any sudden movements, then raised a hand to touch Tali's cheek. Faster than the eye could follow, Tali snatched the woman's hand and squeezed.

"I mean you no harm, child. I just wanted to touch you. Feel your power."

"Tali not know elf. No touch." She released the elf and looked to me for guidance.

"That's rather too intimate a gesture for a stranger," I told her.

"Again, I apologize. I am in awe of you, Tali. I have witnessed several of your exploits. You may not know it, but we have access to your world and you are quite the star."

"Is with cameras?"

"Yes, something like that. But there is no more time for idle chit-chat. I come with a warning. Stay away from Eleron and his foolish friends. They will destroy what I have worked towards. The time will come when you may have no choice, and when it does, request an audience with Rhyadid as is your right. There," she laughed, "now you have some of my power. Remember, it is your right. Fight, but don't risk your life. It is too precious to all of us."

Before I could speak, she was gone.

"Was nice elf?"

"I wish I knew. What the fuck was that about? That was a lame warning. But I guess if we have to, we can use her name and see what effect it has. Who was she?"

"Big boss, maybe?" suggested Tali with a disinterested shrug.

"She might be. Sounds like there are problems in paradise, though. Okay, we need to move. I don't know where, but if she found us so easily, I'm guessing others will be along soon enough."

"Must wait. Charles come."

"How do you know?" I asked, suddenly super-alert.

Tali merely pointed.

I joined her, and looked where she was indicating to see a pinprick of darkness grow rapidly. A portal was opening!

It quickly expanded to afford a glimpse of green grass, the lights of the compound, and trees. Trees! My trees! And there were Charles and Shi, talking to each other as they stared into the portal from the other side. Shi waved, smiling broadly, and Charles nodded to us as the portal became large enough to step through.

Just as I was about to guide Tali home, Charles and Shi rushed to greet us, forcing us to step back as the opening grew to accommodate them.

"You made it," I gasped, hardly able to believe this was happening.

"Tali happy to see friends."

"And we're happy to see you, my dear," beamed Charles, looking exactly as he had when we'd left yesterday.

"You two look like you've been having fun," noted Shi with a wry smile, indicating with his head my stained clothes covered in the green blood of the ceph. "How'd that happen?"

"What do you mean? We thought you were out of time and we were stranded. How did you make it back? Isn't the time up?"

Charles and Shi exchanged a look, then realization dawned. "We've only been apart a few minutes," said Charles. "You both ran through the portal, so I opened it straight back up and we came to get you. But that's not the case for you, I see. What happened?"

"We waited, but you didn't come, so we moved back into the woods when others came across the lake. They were after us, so we kept on moving and found ourselves at the mountain on the map. We've seen it before, when we came through to get you back, remember?"

"This is the same place? Damn, I'd overlooked that. Then what?"

"Then we moved into the mountain, climbed up a ton of steps, slept, and things got pretty wild this morning."

"Really?"

"Can we save the stories for when we get home?" snapped Shi. "It's great to see you and all, but it's literally been a couple of minutes for us. Let's get out of here and close this bloody portal for good."

"Good advice," said Charles.

"Are you both coming, or did you forget anything else?" he asked with a smile.

"Tali has Bear," she said seriously, clutching the teddy to her chest.

"Great, you have Bear. Now let's leave."

Charles put a thumb to the brooch and the closing portal expanded. Wild sparks danced from its edges like a blazing sun and I sighed with longing to get home.

I felt Tali's charged touch as her fingers laced through mine and turned to her.

"What's wrong?"

"Will have to come back?" Her hand squeezed mine tightly.

"No, not if I can help it. What is it?"

"Worry Kifo likes it here. With special lake and beautiful elf woman."

"You aren't jealous, are you?"

"What is jealous?"

"We can discuss it when we get home. Come on, let's go."

"I'll take that," said a familiar voice as the portal imploded and I was grabbed from behind as Eleron snatched the brooch from Charles' extended hand.

"You have got to be kidding me," I sighed.

Tali growled as I was yanked away from her, and she shrieked as her eyes became two bloody orbs and launched at Eleron.

He slammed a fist into her head with a grunt, then grimaced as he made contact. Tali hardly even felt it and smashed a delicate hand into his face, bursting his nose and dislodging several teeth.

With my captors distracted, I rammed my elbow into whoever was behind me and with an *oomph* the hold lessened. I whacked my head back and made contact with a satisfying crunch, then shook their hold free and yanked out Ziggy.

Charles dodged a fist to the face, sidestepped as an elf swung a shortsword at his stomach, and laughed as Shi roared and charged the attacker, tackling him to the ground as my own assailant smiled at me.

"You again," I hissed at Eleron as he backhanded Tali, as much an insult to me as to her.

Tali shrieked, a piercing wail that rang out up and down the valley. She hissed as she morphed, then came up behind Eleron and gripped his neck tight with both hands and squeezed. He turned puce instantly as Tali's incredible power began to crush his windpipe. But then he morphed and she was left holding nothing but air.

Shi's opponent vanished too, and for a moment so did mine, leaving us startled and unsure what to do next.

We had no time to discuss matters, as in the next moment all three elves returned and held various weapons to Charles' throat.

"You dare steal from us?" hissed Eleron. "Take what isn't for you, mongrel, would you? Now you will die as you were supposed to."

Tali started forward, but I warned, "No, don't," and she paused.

"Must protect Charles," she said, turning.

"There's another way." I locked eyes with Eleron and said, "I request an audience with Rhyadid. We accept we are your prisoners, but this is our right. She watches, she listens. She knows." I had no idea if she did, but what was there to lose?

The elves paused, their swords and daggers still at Charles' neck, but none dared kill him.

As if on cue, a small silver drone descended and circled us, before another joined it and hovered before Eleron. He cursed in elvish before acknowledging the drones with a nod.

"What's that all about?" asked Shi, as shocked as Charles by the sudden turn of events.

"We met someone," I said, shrugging, not wanting to give much away.

"You spoke with Rhyadid?" asked one of the elves.

"That's my business. But it is our right and we have witnesses. You will take us to her. We are entitled."

"You are entitled to nothing," hissed Eleron's other accomplice, and he moved his arm to slit Charles' throat.

"No!" commanded Eleron, casting a wary eye at the drones. "Wait! They have the right, and we can't disobey. Not now. But be warned, all of you. You are our prisoners. If you try to escape, or attack, then we may defend ourselves. You invoke an audience, but beware of the consequences. Bind them," he ordered.

Several minutes later, we had our weapons confiscated, and our hands were bound behind our backs with a fine sliver cord that Eleron helpfully explained was unbreakable, and could only be released with their equivalent of whispers. I'd never seen or heard them use any such thing, but figured now wasn't the time for an interrogation.

With unnecessary force, we were shoved up the beach and told to follow the lead elf into the woods.

"What now?" whispered Shi.

"No talking," ordered Eleron from behind as he slammed the butt of his shortsword into Shi's head. He stumbled, but remained silent and kept his footing.

Tali was ahead of me, Charles at the front, so there was no chance of a quiet word for me to explain, but I hoped they would take on trust what I'd done. Not that we now had any choice in the matter.

We followed a track different to the one Tali and I had taken, heading in the same direction by a more direct route, and soon enough we emerged from the trees into a clearing closer to the lake than we had the day before.

The lead elf stopped, and Eleron came from behind to discuss something with him, leaving just the one watching over us. We bunched together and Charles asked, "Who is this Rhyadid?"

"I don't know. She visited us just before you arrived and said to use her name if we needed it. She's obviously got some clout. I didn't know what else to do. But if you can get us out of here, I'm all for it. She's no angel, and likes to keep exotic animals. I don't want to be put into a bloody zoo."

"Tali not zoo animal," she hissed, eyes darkening.

"I know what to do. If it works, grab the brooch. Eleron has it. If not, I'm guessing we have nothing to lose. I'll be as quick as I can, but trust me, okay?"

We nodded, and with that, Shi darted off back into the forest, eating up the space between us and the dense cover in seconds.

"Wait!" shouted the elf watching us, but Shi was already gone.

Eleron and the other elf spun at the commotion and he stormed over, smashed a fist into the lax guard's face, then ordered him to go and retrieve Shi.

The bruised, angry elf loped off after my father, then stopped dead in his tracks as a howl reverberated through the trees.

The cry of the wolf.

"Was that Shi?" I asked Charles.

"It sounds like his call. I'm guessing the lake healed him of his affliction and now he can shape-shift at will like he was always meant to."

"What about his bonds?"

"I don't have all the answers."

"No, of course. What now?"

"Now we wait."

"No talking," snarled Eleron as he punched Charles in the stomach. As he doubled over, Eleron barked out, "You broke your promise. You deserve no audience now. If prisoners try to escape, we have every right to retrieve them by whatever means necessary. You are his accomplices, so will meet the same swift fate."

The drones sank low and danced around Eleron, but he grabbed one and held it up to his face. "You know the law. We have the right. They sully your name and are treacherous. They are not to be trusted. It is to protect you." Eleron nodded to his remaining partner, who lifted his shortsword and swung at Charles' neck, clearly intending to decapitate him.

At the same moment, Shi, or what I assumed was Shi, erupted from the forest then morphed directly in front of the swinging elf and bowled him over. He bounded away then turned. The immense form of an oversized wolf snarled, head low, back rigid, eyes locked on the elves.

He was no longer a tormented beast, neither one thing nor the other. Shi radiated power and wellbeing, a pure wolf three times the size of the regular animal. His coat shone, the dark fur peppered with white around the muzzle like his own hair, but there the similarities ended.

Shi growled in warning again as Eleron drew his sword and shifted to use Charles as a shield. But his movements were too slow compared to Shi's, and the wolf sprang between them, knocking the sword to the ground even as Eleron morphed away and came up next to his weapon. He retrieved it and turned to face the wolf.

The third elf raced back from the woods, took a moment to understand the scene, then sprinted forward and sprang at Charles as the other two went for Shi.

Left alone, Tali and I tried to free ourselves, but the bonds were impossible to break. Panicked, not knowing if it would work, I nevertheless let whispers seep into the rope. With utter focus despite the urgency, I concentrated on the building whisper until I felt a tug in my mind. Connections made, I deepened the magic, repeating the simple spell over and over as I became the strange bindings. With a click in my head, I felt them unravel. Tali's, then Charles' did the same, and we were able to defend ourselves.

Problem being, we had no weapons.

Mace to Meet You

Tali wasted no time. Morphing behind Eleron, she grabbed his head with every intention of ripping it off. But the wily elf morphed and came up behind Shi with his sword already slicing.

Shi, senses heightened, turned and snapped at Eleron's shin before darting past, confounding the elf who spun to face him while Tali returned to my side.

Charles was already in action, kicking and punching at one elf while Tali and I teased the other from the front and behind. But he was adept with his sword, and without a weapon close-quarter combat was extremely risky.

"Come get me, you pointy-eared freak," I taunted.

Distracted, the elf charged forward and Tali took the opportunity to grab Ziggy and throw him to me. I caught the club just as the elf's sword arced, and parried with the dense wood while Tali jumped on his back and dug her thumbs deep into his eyes.

Blinded, he screamed out, spinning to dislodge her. But Tali was a true fighter and refused to let go. The elf slammed back onto the ground, taking the air from Tali's human lungs, and her grip faltered. Eleron thrust down with his shortsword, but his actions were futile as Tali was not human and never would be—something I had to remind myself of—and the blade slid off her precious body like water flowing over rock.

With his sword stuck deep in the ground after such a powerful strike, Eleron tried to tug it free as Tali leaped to her feet and pummeled the shocked elf's face and body in a frenzy.

My own attacker ignored all this, and I had to focus on him as he grinned happily and brushed a golden lock from his face before he thrust, swung, and hacked with his sword in an impressive feat of swordsmanship. I was reduced to merely parrying, no time to attack, and let him drive me back to the rock wall behind me. Pinned to the mountain, I let panic fill my eyes, and lowered Ziggy as if in surrender. The elf smiled slyly, as though he had no intention of showing the restraint he should. It seemed we'd broken our promise and were now nothing but sport.

He thrust out. I danced aside, anticipating what was a sloppy move, and as his sword tip shattered against the rock, I willed Ziggy into a spiked mace on a chunky chain and swung the weighted weapon right into his torso. With the wind knocked out of him, I slammed the mace into his arm, expecting bone to break, but these damn elves were tough, and he merely snarled. He made a break for it, but Ziggy had other ideas and I swung low, tripping him and gouging his leg. As he jumped up, I danced behind him and snapped his sword arm behind his back and grabbed the other with a quick morph then wrapped the elven rope around his wrists. It cinched tight of its own accord and knotted as though following my will.

As the elf cursed, I chased back into the fight, retrieving the fallen bonds as I went.

One elf was fighting Shi, and Eleron was laughing as he battled Tali and Charles. There was no denying their proficiency, but their self-confidence made them careless and they made risky moves, depending on their apparent ability to recover from wounds rapidly to compensate for any errors. Charles had his daggers now, and with one in each hand, he crouched to protect his belly as he circled Eleron and jabbed out when opportunity arose. Tali circled behind, repeatedly trying to trip the smarmy elf who fought like he had eyes in the back of his head.

Certain they could deal with Eleron, I skirted around then snuck up behind the other elf as he focused on the snarling, wild form of Shi. There was now no denying the water had worked its miracle and he was cured. Was this what he'd wanted? To be able to still shift into the wolf? Or had he desired a total end to his shape-shifting abilities? I assumed the water gave you what you desired, or were capable of, but my guess was yes, he wanted this. The animal was too deeply-rooted in his system, his very being, to ever be banished for good, so this was the best compromise Lake Elinor was able to offer.

Shi feinted left then darted right as the elf moved to attack, and nipped at the side of his foe, sinking his teeth deep into an exposed underarm. He tore a ragged lump of flesh and spat it out as the elf grunted in pain but spun and caught Shi a glancing blow across the flank. Shi tumbled aside then righted and snarled at the elf as I crept up behind and slapped the rope over his free hand. Instantly, it wrapped tight and the end sprang like a snake, caught his sword arm, and dragged it behind his back before tying tight.

The elf squirmed and swore, but the binding held fast as Shi circled the prisoner, passing in front of me and locking his gaze on mine.

There was intelligence behind the eyes of the wolf now. He wasn't just a wild animal. He knew himself and he knew me. Shi nodded, and I grinned, then we left the struggling elf and turned to assist Charles and Tali.

Only to find a dozen armored guards standing patiently as if waiting for us to finish our game of tease-the-elf.

As everyone became aware that something was up, the fighting slowed then stopped and we grouped together to face the new threat. Eleron and his team seemed as concerned by this new turn of events as us, but remained silent as they helped one another escape the bonds. They fell away easily enough under the instruction of Eleron, and he snapped what I understood were insults at them under his breath, never taking his eyes off the drone that hovered in front of the stoic guards.

"What now?" I whispered to Charles.

"Now, I do believe we are at the mercy of forces as yet unseen. We might learn something, so stand down, and that goes for you too, Tali."

Somehow still clutching Bear, Tali smiled demurely and asked, "Not kill elves?"

"Not right now, my dear. Maybe later?"

Tali nodded, satisfied with this.

Shi approached, growling at the guards, and they shifted position for the first time as they raised their swords as one. There wasn't even a flicker of expression on their determined faces.

The wolf calmed, reading the situation, and as his breathing slowed so the animal became the man. Shi grunted as he moved from his position on all fours to standing, then grinned at us and said, "The lake cured me! That's incredible. I can shape-shift any time, even here. Awesome! And I was still me. I could think straight and do what I wanted, not just blindly attack anything in sight. It's been so long, with so much pain caused. I can't believe it." A tear fell; he made no move to wipe it away. How deeply this must be affecting him after almost a century of nigh on unbearable pain every month and the things he'd done when in his shifted form. I couldn't even begin to imagine the relief he felt.

"We're very happy for you," I said, "but you might want to ask if you can get some clothes."

Shi glanced down and noted he was naked for the first time. He chuckled, then called out, "Can I get something to wear? I don't want you guys ogling me. It's weird."

"Not much to ogle," grunted a surly elf as he stepped forward with a simple pair of trousers and a very nice dark green shirt.

"Way to give a guy a complex," grumbled Shi as he took the clothes with a nod then dressed quickly.

"You seem to be very prepared," noted Charles.

"We have orders. We were told what to expect," he said with a shrug. "Now, you will come with us." He glared at Eleron and his buddies and added, "All of you."

Eleron sneered, but made no move to defy the commander of the guards.

There was little in the way of choice unless we were prepared to let Tali return to her true form and burn them all, but that seemed like a very bad idea when we were still stuck here and not in immediate danger. Maybe we'd just get a rap on the knuckles and be sent on our way? It was wishful thinking, and I didn't for one moment expect that to happen, but at least we weren't being attacked, so for now that would have to be good enough.

Should kill elves? asked Tali into my head.

Not yet. Let's wait and see what happens. These guards are under orders to take us somewhere, and I think I know where, so for now just go along with it.

If try to hurt us will kill. Can become dragon again then?

Yes. If they try anything, destroy them.

I felt satisfaction radiate into my mind. Tali lived for the hunt, and she lived to protect her family.

The contingent of guards moved in and we were marched around the perimeter of the mountain, heading back towards the lake. The ground was rough, with numerous outcroppings and small pools we had to traverse, but the guards seemed to be in no rush and took a leisurely, almost relaxed pace. The underlying threat of violence remained, and I was certain that if we tried anything they wouldn't hesitate to do whatever it took to get us back in line.

Eleron and his cohorts didn't object. They were ahead of us, but didn't try to talk to the guard or break the formation, just sauntered along with the usual cocky attitude every elf I'd met seemed to have. It was difficult to accept that I, too, had this blood running through my veins. Sure, it was diluted, but it was there nevertheless.

Shi had it too, and Charles was half-elf. Was this why we were so confident and self-assured? Was it our ancestry? The fact this elf, Eleron, was family? I chuckled at the thought. He was my what, great-grandfather? Shi's grandfather? Just like Charles was mine. It was ridiculous. We were family and he wanted to destroy us. Charles the most, because it reflected badly on him? How cold, callous, and cruel could he be?

Is who we become the result of nature or nurture? Were we distant from others, maybe sometimes even disdainful, and shunned much of humanity because we were part elf? Or was it because we were like all other human Necros and had been forced to face the brutal side of ourselves so often that we couldn't cope with the mundane world most of our species lived in? I believed it was the latter, but seeing Eleron again and the way he was made me doubt everything I had ever believed, and it made me furious. He would rather see his own flesh and blood dead than accept his son as his own. His time would come, I'd make sure of it.

Coming out of my dark reverie, I realized we had stopped. We were beside a wide staircase carved into the rock, very different to the one Tali and I had climbed the previous day. The steps led up to a large veranda, and without instruction we were prodded from behind so followed the lead guard up.

At the veranda, elves stared at us as we passed ornate pillars holding up a domed roof, then took another set of stairs. The higher we went, the more elves we encountered. Most of them dressed in similar plain but tastefully decorated clothes of light colors, some with weapons held by leather and silver belts and holsters, many of the women with delicate webs of silver ornamentation woven expertly through their long hair. Every single one was beautiful, and the smell as we crossed paths on the stairs made me go weak at the knees.

Shi stumbled as we passed a group of three females close enough to reach out and touch them, and I had to resist the urge to stop and admire their beauty as it became almost overwhelming.

How could such beautiful, self-aware lifeforms be so cold and cruel? How had they achieved so much when they had zero empathy and seemingly no sense of duty to their own kind?

Did I give a shit? No, I fucking did not. They could burn for all I cared, because the more of them we passed, and the more I studied their facial expressions, the more evident it became that they really did think nothing of us at all. Not beyond an excited curiosity about us being here, and the chance to get close to the filthy humans they seemingly enjoyed watching murder each other.

Another balcony, this time open to the elements, with a robust gathering of inquisitive elves in small groups who stopped talking the moment we stepped onto the spotless marble. They giggled, or oohed and aahed as we passed without pause, the guards grouping tight together to ensure nobody could run. Where we'd go I had no idea, but they seemed to think it was a risk so acted accordingly.

The proximity of so many was playing havoc with my mind and body, and it was clear I wasn't alone. Shi kept stumbling, then gasping as he breathed in their scent, and Charles lost his rigid posture and merely bumbled along, every step seemingly a struggle. My head swam with their perfume, with their sheer loveliness, and their chatter became a seductive song in my head like a siren calling me to the deep.

We all breathed a sigh of relief when we left the gathering behind and moved up yet another series of steps past small houses and more pavilions and verandas.

The view out into the valley and lake below was just as beautiful as from the air. A sudden and brief shower caused everything to sparkle in the gentle sunlight shining down from a clear, slightly unbalanced sky. What was it about the sky? The colors were off somehow. It was blue, but no blue I had ever encountered. What did that mean for the atmosphere? It was obviously breathable, but was there more oxygen? Was that why they were taller than humans? Slightly more fine-boned? I was no anthropologist, but there were definitely differences between the two races, even if only slight.

As we ascended this main thoroughfare, the more elves we encountered. Seemingly, word had spread, no doubt aided by our escapade earlier. To be fair, you couldn't exactly have missed it. Seemed there were more houses up here, and more inquisitive elves, and the dress style changed too. These clowns were pompous, preening fools more interested in showing themselves off than in us. A courtly contingent, the wealthy, more empowered ones who clung to their positions and lorded it over the others? What were they called in the old days back home? Twats! Yes, that was it. A bunch of elven twats.

Finally, we were led onto a large platform with ornate railings, affording a magnificent, uninterrupted view of the valley and lake, and because of its protruding position, of the numerous buildings on the mountain itself. Above were the uppermost parts of the castle, with serpentine streets and steps leading to what I assumed were homes within the walls protected by guards.

The covered porch led back into the castle proper by several doors hung with rich red curtains, and centered between them was an ornate silver chair with so much detailed work I didn't know where to begin looking. A red velvet cushion shone like freshly spilled blood. A simple table beside it held a pitcher of sparkling water and a crystal glass.

A guard went through a curtain then returned a moment later and held it aside. It was the woman we'd met earlier. Her dragon appeared from where it had been hiding behind her neck, then sat on her shoulder and peered at us with interest. She thanked the guard before he returned to his post, then sat in the chair and studied us in turn, frowning when she cast her gaze on Eleron and his friends.

"Positions as discussed," she said sweetly to the guards.

We were split into two, elves one side, us the other, with two guards between us to keep the distance. Guess she thought there might be trouble.

"Now, here we are at last," she said with a smile which I couldn't decide was welcoming and amused, or cold and calculating.

We were either going to live or die. Seemingly, it was up to her.

Queen

The three elves we'd dealt with so far were annoyingly perfect. Their essence was intoxicating, and if you didn't keep a tight hold of your own mind you'd do their bidding and follow them willingly through the Gates of Hell. Their smell was sweeter than any perfume, their auras shone with promises of delight, and they radiated an almost divine presence. But underlying it all was a bitterness. A realization that they weren't these pure creatures myth and legend would have us believe. Rather, they were cold, calculating, pompous, and cared less than nothing for us.

But as we stood in the presence of this woman, I felt only her beauty and power. There was no malevolence, no desire to hurt us, no sinister undertone. She exuded a serene melancholy, an acceptance of her own limitations, and yet absolute confidence in who, and what, she was. She was an open book, revealing her inner self, and I understood that although it would pain her, she wouldn't hesitate to destroy us if she felt threatened or believed it would be for the good of her people.

"Who are you?" asked Charles, although he clearly had his suspicions.

"A queen amongst many queens, is the best equivalent I can use in your human tongue. Do you not recognize one when you see one?"

"I do. It is a pleasure to meet you."

"My name is Rhyadid. I know all of you, and it is with a warm heart I welcome you."

"I didn't think elves had warm hearts," growled Shi. "The ones we've met are cold as ice."

Rhyadid chuckled, pale eyes dancing with amusement. But they weren't regular eyes any more, they were the eyes of a witch, one who in our world had access to her sisters—the long line of witches of her lineage. Like a goat's, with horizontal pupils, it signified one who was marked as special for her abilities.

"What's so funny?" asked Shi.

"That you would base your opinion of a whole species on three foolish, desperate males."

"Who are you calling foolish?" growled Eleron as he advanced, his shortsword clanging against his lightweight ceremonial chainmail.

"One who was defeated by a human before in our arena, and had his head stomped into mush by a dragon. Who had to be collected in pieces and left in a net for an entire year before his body reformed to become whole again. Who was banned as all elves now are from the human realm, but was given special permission in order to eradicate his bastard, mongrel offspring. And who failed at even that," she laughed, lifting her head up to reveal a perfect neck.

"That's not the whole story, and you know it," snapped Eleron, anger surfacing as his fingers tightened around his shortsword's grip.

The guard stepped forward, reaching for his own sword, but Rhyadid put her hand to the elf's shoulder and he waited for further instruction.

"Eleron, be still. You shame yourself and us with your unseemly display of anger. You were sent to destroy this man, but instead you and your foolish compatriots managed to lose a brooch. How ridiculous." She laughed again, then her face grew serious. "Be gone, and know this, Eleron. Your chance to put down your half-elf offspring has passed, and you will not interfere in human affairs again. The ban is absolute once more. No elf will venture into the human world for fear of the punishment you will face. There will be no resurrection beyond enough to let you live out an eternity of endless purgatory here. You will be neither alive nor dead, merely suffer for your treachery. Be gone!" Rhyadid nodded to her guard. The twelve men in full armor stepped forward.

Eleron turned as they marched him and his two companions away and growled, "You'll pay for this. Nobody tells me what to do. Not even the queen of this isle." They were led away, leaving us dumbfounded and unsure of our own future.

"You're the queen of an island?" asked Charles, intrigued the same as we all were.

"Indeed. I won't bore you with our geography, but yes, I rule here. But I do not wield the power as I should, as is my right, and creatures such as Eleron, that despicable thing, have more say than I would rather in our society. He comes from a powerful family with much interest in our affairs, and there is, shall we say, animosity. I would not have had him come for you, to murder his own child, but it was out of my hands. Please accept my apologies."

"I do," said Charles keenly.

"Thank you. Eleron was banned, as all elves are, but in recent years there have been allowances made for forays into your realm, and there always have been. Special permissions. We knew nothing of your existence, but once you were discovered, he was sent back by a vote and there was nothing I could do to stop it. He failed, thankfully, but I think you are smarter than my brethren believe. You planned for his return, did you not?"

"We might have had a little plan," Charles laughed.

"Indeed. To steal a brooch and open a portal so you could heal your own son. How very touching. And now here you are, having been captured once again, at the mercy of a queen without a kingdom truly of her own. Without a crown that would see her sit on the throne and fulfill her destiny."

"You knew of my plans, didn't you?" asked Charles, clearly understanding what was going on better than the rest of us.

"What makes you say that?" she asked, cocking her head to the side.

"If you have any authority at all, and it's clear you do, then you chose to allow Eleron into our world. If you didn't want me dead, then you knew I had a plan to steal the brooch and come here to help my son heal."

"You are certainly of elven descent," said Rhyadid. "Yes, you have caught me in my little game," she chuckled. "I had hoped you would survive. I watched via the drones we have in your world and knew you would come. But know this. I did not interfere in the outcome, or influence your actions. I merely allowed Eleron to chase after you with his foolish friends in the hopes that you would show him what you were made of. And you have. All of you."

"So you wanted us to come?" I asked. "Why?"

"The answer to that is twofold. One, to prove I was right and the ban on us coming to your world should now be absolute. Too much interference has altered the course of your history already. You have some of our technology when you should have discovered your own when the time was right. And look at the utter mess you have made of your world because of it. That is our doing. We hold the blame. You weren't ready for such technological progress. Two, so you can go somewhere else where an elf of pure blood absolutely cannot. It has always been prohibited, and there are no exceptions. Not because we cannot venture there, there is no need for a dragon companion, for instance, but because if we ever set foot in the dwarves' kingdom, or they in ours, there would be war."

"But I'm a half-elf, and my family has elven blood too."

"No matter. You are not true elves, and you were born and raised in your world. You are more human than elf, and that will always be the case."

"So you want us to do something for you?" I asked.

"Indeed. As I mentioned, there is a crown to be restored to its rightful owner. Me. Lost long ago, it has been the cause of much turmoil and unrest here since it was taken. Now you must retrieve it for us." The dragon wyrmling on her shoulder stirred, its long tail swishing as it stretched out then opened a lazy eye and peered at us sleepily.

"Why should we?" asked Shi, about as keen as I was to embark on another adventure.

"Why? Because I ask it of you," she said, a gentle smile spreading across her perfect face.

"Tali not like cold places under earth. Smell funny, and lots of little men making noise. Is like being in big house. No sky."

"No, there is no sky, but there are shafts that let in the light from the human world to that of the dwarves'. But you are correct, Tali, it does smell funny, apparently."

"That isn't a reason for us to go," I said. "We just want to return home."

"Then why don't you leave and go about your lives?" she asked. "But if you accept this request, I will be forever in your debt. You are Necros, and will live many years if you don't get yourselves killed first. Wouldn't it be sensible to know you have the enduring gratitude of a true Elf Queen? I'm sure the favor can be repaid one day, and surely that is worthwhile?"

"So if we do this thing for you, you're in our debt?" asked Shi.

"Yes."

"And you will be what, the real queen of this island, wherever it is, however large it is?"

"Yes. Please don't ask for more detail, you shall receive none. This is still our home, and humans cannot know more than I am willing to share. I know you have your maps, but they are local to this zone, and do not give the full picture. Will you accept?"

"Do we have a choice in this?" I asked, realizing that for all her sweetness and good humor she was still an elf, and I didn't believe that she was much different to Eleron. She was playing a game, much like Eloise played hers. Power struggles and politics, it was the bloody same wherever you went. It made me sick.

Rhyadid looked at each of us in turn, then she simply burst out laughing. Her cheeks burned pink as she was overcome with mirth, and reveled in her clear delight at the question.

"A choice?" she finally said. "You ask if you have a choice? My dear human, have you learned nothing yet? There are nothing but choices. You may always choose. You may decide to deny my request, or try to kill me right this very moment—" her guards stiffened, but she put a hand up to still them, "—with your magical weapon, Ziggy, or you may try to cheat me out of what is mine. There are nothing but choices."

"And if we choose not to accept your quest?" asked Charles.

"Why, then I will kill you all right here."

"Oh, so you aren't as nice as you act?" I said.

"Nice? I am nice. I am in all likelihood the kindest, most generous elf you are ever likely to meet. But that does not mean I will be taken for a fool. I am a queen and I will be treated as such. You are human, are you not?" she asked, focusing on me.

"Yes."

"And Tali is a dragon?"

"Again, yes."

"Much as Nava is a painted dog, and lovely Mai is a gnome. We each have our nature, and we each must accept our role in this charade we call life. I am an elf, and a queen who demands the respect she deserves. I have saved you from the ignominy of being killed by the fool Eleron and his cohorts. Does that not deserve gratitude and servility?"

"Gratitude yes. But I bow to no man or woman under duress," I said, holding her gaze, unflinching.

"Then learn to bow!" she hissed, eyes cold and hard. "Nobody is without a master or mistress. Each of us answers to somebody."

"Even you?"

"Of course. Those fools at court, the council, endless rules and regulations. It is so tiresome. But I will have my crown, and I will at least have my proper position as ruler where I can make the decisions and they will show due respect."

"How do we know you will keep your word?" asked Charles. "What's to stop you coming and killing us in our sleep with one of your brooches?"

"The brooches will be useless after today."

"But there are more?"

"Of course."

"So my question stands. You say the ban on your kind visiting us will be absolute, but it doesn't seem like you can promise that."

"Nobody else has any interest in you, and Eleron knows his place. He will not try to harm you again."

"I meant you, not Eleron."

"Because I give you my word. That is enough."

"Then I accept," said Charles. "But not Mai or Nava. They make no promise to you. As to my son and grandson, and Tali, they make their own decisions."

"As you wish," said Rhyadid. "The gnome and dog are free of this request. What say the rest of you?"

"I agree," I said immediately.

"You do?" asked Shi, eyes wide.

"Like we have a choice."

"What if she's lying?"

"She isn't lying," said Charles. "I can tell. Can't you?"

Shi's shoulders slumped. "Yeah, you're right. I believe her. Fine, I accept."

We turned to Tali, who had remained motionless and utterly silent throughout the rest of the conversation.

"Tali, this is entirely up to you. Make your own decision and don't feel pressured," I said.

"Will do what elf want," she said, eyes boring into Rhyadid.

"Are you sure?"

"Yes. But if she cheat, or hurt friends, will kill. Will burn elf and all with her."

The guard were instantly advancing, and Tali hissed as she stepped forward to do battle.

"Enough. Leave her be," ordered Rhyadid, smiling.

The guard retreated to her side, hands remaining on their shortswords. Tali took a step back, shoulders squared, eyes burning with dislike.

"I admire your courage and loyalty, but there is no need for such animosity. If you fulfill my request, all will be well."

"I still don't understand," I admitted. "How will a crown change anything? It's just a symbol of a position, nothing more."

"You are very wrong," said Rhyadid. "It is more than that. Only a true queen may wear it. This is no trinket, no mere icon. It holds real command. Shall we say, it is compelling? Elves have lost many of the ancient arts we learned from the dwarves long ago. We can no longer make weapons with the potency they used to contain, but we still have the ability to create magical items beyond your wildest dreams, and have technology you could never imagine. The crown was forged thirty thousand years ago and was always more powerful than any other item ever made in our world."

"That's when humans were still in caves."

"Yes, there were merely a handful of you then, and you had no agriculture, no weapons beyond flint and wood, and wandered like lost children. But we were at our zenith, and had good relations with the dwarves. But as with all such things, they pass, and there was a change in the dynamic. A falling out occurred, and the relationship between our two species became tense, then faltered, and eventually collapsed. This was long ago, the truth of it all lost to history and time, but one of their final acts of treachery was to take back the crown they helped us forge, and it severed our relationship for good."

"And you want us to steal back what was stolen from you?" I asked.

"I do. With it, I will have the respect of all elves and the power it contains will be mine."

"What power is that, may I ask?" said Charles, utterly focused on this enigmatic elf.

"Understand, I owe you no explanation. You have been told more than most elves know. Don't take me for a fool. Just know the crown is the key to my position and that I saved your lives."

"You set us up," shouted Shi. "You knew what we were doing and how we planned to get here and just watched and hoped we'd beat Eleron and get the brooch. Then you set him loose so he'd bring us here so you could get this damn crown."

"Be that as it may, and I must congratulate you as I honestly didn't think you'd get this far, the fact remains I did stop Eleron killing you all. Maybe you would have defeated him, but it's doubtful. He knew you would use the brooch, so has been waiting for you."

"So you let us do this hoping we'd succeed so you could use us?" I asked.

"Of course. This is how things are. You play a part. Now, was there anything else?"

"Just a few details," said Charles amiably. "Like where we have to go, how we get there, and what this crown looks like. A picture would help. And what is it called? Does it have a name?"

"All crowns have names," said Rhyadid. "All pertinent information is contained within the sphere." Rhyadid lifted an arm so her wide sleeve parted. A small silver orb drifted out then hovered at eye level. With a nod from her, it spun, then glided over to Charles who opened his palm and let the globe settle. It shrank until the size of an eyeball, much to his delight. He placed it in his inner jacket pocket.

"Cool," gasped Shi.

"Now, I believe you have something of mine?" she said, glaring at Eleron as he was marched back into the room alone.

"What?" he asked.

"The brooch," she said sweetly, eyes saying the opposite.

"Oh, ha, yes, of course."

"How will we get home?" I asked.

"I will open the portal for you. Remember, no more elves will come to your realm, and humans may not venture here, not that you have ever been allowed. Come, approach me."

Eleron walked forward, confident as always, and when close enough, and with the guard on high alert, he dropped the brooch into Rhyadid's palm. She reached into her sleeve and stowed away our ticket out of this mad place. Eleron was marched off.

"We shall never meet again, at least I hope not. When, or if, you succeed, a portal will open for the crown to be sent through. That is all." With a wave of her hand, she turned and walked back into the opulent interior. The guard filed out, leaving us alone on the dizzying heights of this magnificent mountain.

"That was weird," said Shi, hitching up his jeans.

"Weird? That's all you have to say?" I asked, incredulous.

"What? It was. Very bloody weird."

"It was," I admitted. "Beyond weird. So, we're really going on a quest to get some old crown for a mad elf queen?"

"I don't believe we have a choice in the matter," said Charles.

"Tali not like elf."

"None of us did," I said.

Charles opened his mouth to speak, but his words were taken from the air as a portal snapped into existence and expanded rapidly to fill the space between us and the railing. It was my home. The house looked so normal that I could have broken down and cried. Like none of this insanity had happened.

With no reason to stay, and with everyone amazed we'd actually made it, we stepped from one bewildering world into another.

Never Ending Games

The moment we were through the portal, it winked out of existence. We stood there, mute and motionless, hardly able to believe we'd made it back. Charles and Shi were the first to move, leaving Tali and me holding hands as we came to terms with being back where we belonged. Hardly any time at all had passed for the others, but the extra day Tali and I had spent with the elves had left its mark on our psyche. Slowly, we adjusted, and took our first tentative steps.

"Grass feel nice. Is proper grass. Not funny elf kind," said Tali as she wriggled her toes in a most lovely manner.

"And the air's different. Heavier, but it feels right."

Then the spell was broken and the world truly came flooding back in.

"We made it!" I whooped, then took Tali in my arms and spun her in a circle, laughing as she beamed at me.

"Did good?"

"Yes, you did great. I'm so proud of you." I slowed, then lowered Tali, but I didn't release her. Without thinking about it, I kissed her on the lips. Tali responded, and I knew this was right. That we were destined to be together, and although it wasn't conventional, there was no fighting what was clearly inevitable.

The world, our world, faded away and all that remained was Tali and me. Her soft, warm lips tight against mine, the heat of her body pressed into me, and her fingers tracing lines along my back.

Whatever the future held it would be ours, together, and in that kiss a new bond was formed. Yes, we were different, and yes, we would face difficulties, but when you know that other person is your soul mate why would you even try to resist? Life was hard enough without putting obstacles in your own way.

Charles coughed discreetly; we broke our embrace to find him and Shi beaming at us.

"Are happy?" Tali asked me, head cocked to the side.

"Very."

"And so are we. You two are meant to be together."

"Shi?" I asked.

"You want my opinion?" he asked, surprised.

"Maybe," I laughed, unable to even think straight.

"You only get a few chances at true happiness in this life. I should know. You'd be an utter fool to let the opportunity to share it with someone you love pass you by."

"Thank you," I said.

"Tali loves Kifo," she said, smiling warmly.

Do you really? You know what real love is?

Is when you want to be with someone all the time. Feel funny inside when not there. Think about what are doing?

Yes, it is. Now, do you want to rest? You have been incredible and we couldn't have done it without you. You saved us all.

Always will.

"What are you two talking about?" asked Charles with a wide smile.

"Tali needs to rest. But I was telling her how grateful we are, and that she did incredibly well. We made it! We actually made it. And Shi is healed and I don't know about you guys, but I feel amazing. In the best shape of my life despite the fighting and dealing with the elves."

"Me too," admitted Charles.

"I sense the change inside me," said Shi. "I can shape-shift at will, I'm not beholden to the moon, and I remain in control when I become the wolf. Thank you all. I can't begin to describe how this feels. After a century of purgatory, I feel as though I've been granted a second chance at life. It's because of you. My family."

"Will sleep now. Is good what we did?"

"Very," I said. "We still have things to do, and a lot to discuss, but for now, rest."

With a nod, Tali walked towards the house and changed back into her dragon form as she did so. She shimmered from green to gold then red and back again, radiating happiness and contentment. I felt the same.

It truly was a great day to be alive.

Nava loped over, barking with joy, and nearly bowled me over.

"Hey there. I missed you a lot."

"It's only been a few hours," he chuckled, tail wagging.

"Time's screwy there. We had to spend the night. We had a massive aerial battle with this weird creature, and some crazy adventures. I'll tell you about it later. You look shattered. You doing okay?"

"I'm okay. Just tired. Glad you're home, and that Tali's safe. Let's speak later." With a happy wag, Nava returned to Tali. She was already curled up, and they shared a few words before Nava hunkered in tight to her flank and I felt the joy like a warm fire on a cold winter's evening.

Things were back how they should be. How I wished they'd remain forever.

I grinned manically as I heard the front door slam, and next thing I knew I was on my back with Mai hugging my chest.

"Whoa, take it easy," I chuckled.

"Mai is very happy Kifo is alive. I felt so bad for making Charles lose the brooch, then happy when I found it, then sad, then happy when we came home, then sad again when you went back to that horrid place and the portal closed, and it was just so upsetting."

"Take a breath," I laughed. "It's over with now. We're back and safe. You didn't mean to disrupt the portal, and we figured it out. No need to worry. I missed you so much."

I stood when he hopped off me, then held out my arms and he jumped up and cuddled me. "Mai is happy again. And I saw you with Tali."

"Yes," I said warily. "How does that make you feel?"

"Confused, happy, concerned, and cautious," he said, head bowed.

I put a finger under his chin and lifted until he met my eyes. "That's understandable. And to tell you the truth," I whispered, getting closer, "I feel exactly the same way. Nothing will happen right now, and we have things we need to do as this isn't exactly over yet, but whatever the future holds we remain together, yes?"

"Always," beamed Mai, then he jumped down and dashed back over to Tali and Nava who got the same generous show of affection as he welcomed them home.

Charles, Shi, and I looked at each other, clearly unable to decide what to do, then we simply burst out laughing. The relief was palpable and we didn't know how else to express it.

When the laughter subsided, Charles said, "We actually did the impossible. We went to the elven homeworld and made it back in one piece. You must tell us about your adventure. You really battled in the sky with Tali?"

"Yes, and it was scary as hell. But she was amazing, as always."

"What was all that with Rhyadid, though?" said Shi, suddenly looking very tired.

As the adrenaline wore off, I began to feel the tug of sleep too. I was beyond exhausted, and heading for a mighty comedown after such crazy antics. Even Charles was flagging, his shoulders stooped, hair unruly, which was a sure sign he wasn't himself.

"Let's go sit," suggested Charles.

We gathered around the fire pit and I lit a small fire for comfort. It was then I truly felt like I had returned home. No sooner had we settled than Mai arrived with coffee and cake.

"For my boys," he beamed as he set everything down.

"Did you bake a cake?" I asked, amazed. "When did you have the time?"

"Mai always has time for you," he mumbled, kicking at the dirt.

"Won't you join us?" asked Charles, noting three mugs.

"Things to do. The house is a mess after being away. Busy, busy." Mai dashed off, clearly thinking of other things already.

We sipped the coffee, which I realized might be the last I had, and demolished the cake greedily. It might not have been real chocolate, but it tasted great and boosted my energy levels a little.

"What are we going to do?" asked Shi, relaxed enough that he undid the straps securing his sword behind his back and laid it at his side.

"About?"

"Don't be a dick, Charles," I said.

"Sorry. Old habits. I assume you mean about our new friend, Rhyadid? The queen of who knows what?"

"Of course I bloody do!" scowled Shi, then took a big bite of cake.

"We need to delve deeper and see what we can uncover. How interesting this is. First, we visit the elves, now the dwarves."

"And how do we do that anyway?" I wondered.

"We need to find a dwarf who will open up a tunnel for us."

"And that will lead directly to their world? How? No portals involved? No bloody brooches?"

"No, no brooches. To be truthful, I know less about dwarves than elves, but I know they don't use portals to travel from here to their world. Most don't come here at all. But there are a few. They can, er, make tunnels." Charles shrugged.

"In other words, you're clueless," laughed Shi, spitting cake crumbs everywhere.

"He may be, but I'm not," said a woman from behind me.

Charles and Shi's eyes widened, then Shi sighed and took another bite as I whirled, Ziggy already in my hand.

"Eloise?" I blurted, relaxing my stance but keeping Ziggy gripped tightly.

"Hello everyone. How lovely, coffee and cake. May I join you?" she asked, not waiting for an answer before she sat on a stump, making a show of brushing off the dirt first.

"Did you morph?" I asked, deciding to play it cool and resume my seat.

"Indeed. It's the only way to travel these days," she laughed, her goat eyes boring into mine as if she could read the entire tale of our misadventures that way. I held her gaze, but it wasn't a nice feeling.

"What on earth are you doing here, Eloise?" asked Charles, fidgeting with his jacket lapel.

"Come Charles, you know I like to keep up-to-date on things that interest you."

"Guess that leaves me and Kifo out of the picture then," grumbled Shi as he looked longingly at his sword.

"Don't be so petulant," snapped Eloise, before her face softened and she added, "I'm happy you made it. All of you." Eloise clapped her hands as her face brightened and she studied us each in turn.

"I'm beat. That was epic, guys. Thank you for your help. It means the world to me." Shi stood, and reached for his sword.

"Sit down," said Eloise, face darkening.

"You don't get to tell me what to do," barked Shi, clenching and unclenching his fists and narrowing his eyes as the smoke spiraled.

"Then look at it as a request. I truly am glad you all made it back and that you, Shi, are recovered. I see that you are. How marvelous."

"You can tell by looking at him?" I asked.

"I can. I see that all of you are more than you were. You have elven blood in your veins, so the lake aided you. You will recover better than ever, it will be harder for you to be injured, and I expect your lives are extended too. What lucky men you are."

"Yeah, we're just so bloody fortunate," said Shi, staring at her defiantly.

"Just sit down and let her say what she wants to say," said Charles as he put a hand to Shi's arm.

"Fine." Shi slumped onto the stump and tapped a foot.

"Why are you acting this way?" asked Eloise.

"Because I don't like you interfering in my business. Because you never acted like a proper great-aunt when I was growing up, always trying to get me to do your dirty work, and it got worse when I was an adult. You interfered, you drove a wedge between me and Charles, and you never once tried to help me sort out the one thing that stopped me being happy."

"I apologize if you think I interfered. That wasn't my intention. Not in a bad way. I always wanted what's best for you. For all of you."

"Oh yeah, that why you never lifted a finger to help us with this? Why you let us go and most likely die?"

"I thought you said it would be a breeze," I said. "That we'd be in and out in a few minutes and were sure to succeed?"

"Did I?" he asked, suddenly finding his boots interesting. "Maybe I exaggerated a little. But she knows what I mean. She's a spook, like Charles, but with bloody bells and whistles on. Always trying to find an angle. It drives me crazy."

"Do I drive you crazy?" asked Charles.

"Course you bloody do. You drive us both crazy."

"He's right," I snorted, amused how childish Shi could be for a grown man when confronted with family.

"I suppose I can be somewhat intense, and rather secretive at times," Charles admitted with a sheepish grin.

We laughed, the tension lifted, but then Eloise coughed to focus our attention and the mood darkened again.

"Shi, I am sorry you feel that way, but I have always loved you and always will. We haven't seen one another for the longest time, and I hope that can change from now on. But rest assured, I have been following your progress and getting regular updates from Charles."

"That makes me feel so much better."

"No need for sarcasm. Now, I want to hear about your adventure. But most of all, I want to know if you met Rhyadid and if she asked you to possibly do something for her?"

"For fuck's sake! I knew it. It's not enough that Charles and I manipulated Kifo into helping me, that we kept him in the dark and he only helped save Charles because we wanted the bloody brooch, but this is too much. Charles, were you in on this all along? Is this why you helped me?" Shi was on his feet and close to grabbing his sword.

"What's going on? Shi, what are you talking about? Charles, what does he mean?" I asked, standing and ready to calm Shi down.

Charles stood too, and put an arm to Shi and said, "I don't know what you're talking about."

"She does," said Shi, pointing at Eloise, who remained seated and utterly composed.

We turned to her, and damn it but I raised my eyebrows. Maybe it was catching.

"Please sit, then I will explain."

Shi slumped back down with a grumble, so Charles and I resumed our seats.

"Go on then. This better be good, Aunty," said Charles, grinding his teeth.

Eloise gathered her flowing dress around her like a protective blanket, sniffed, made a gentle whisper so the fire burned a little brighter and the smoke lessened, then said, "A long time ago, I heard of the waters of Elinor. We had always tried our very best to find a cure for you, Shi, but there was nothing to be done. You endured so much heartache and hardship, and even the whispers of many witches and wizards, along with numerous visits from mages of all description. Nothing worked. But when I heard of the possible solution, I told your father. He told you, and you made your strange little deal with him about killing five men if he would help when the time was right."

"We know this," said Charles.

"Just a recap," snapped Eloise. "What I also heard about was the trouble the elves were having. If you think our power-plays are vindictive, then you don't know that race well. They have very strict rules and hierarchies, and tradition plays an important role in their lives. I knew of Rhyadid, and the problems she faced. When I learned of your little plan to go to the elven homeworld, I had hoped that you might bump into her as well."

"Why? And why do I get the feeling you manipulated us?" asked Charles.

"It was your idea to go once you heard about the lake," Eloise reminded him.

"An idea you gave me."

"There was no other solution. It was to help Shi. Nothing more."

"There's always something more with you," said Shi.

"That is actually true," Eloise admitted. "But regardless of that fact, it was the only solution. Things worked out well by chance with Tali. It would make things much easier with her in human form so the timing was definitely right. I merely hoped you might meet the queen and she would ask something of you. Did she?" asked Eloise, obviously feigning innocence.

"I'm sure you already know," I said. "And I'm not impressed with how this is going. What's your agenda here? What did you do?"

"What makes you think I did anything? What makes you think I have an agenda?"

"You always do," said Shi. "Always. Just tell us."

"The elves lost their advanced metallurgy skills. They no longer interact with the dwarves. They need someone to recover a certain crown. Someone who can enter the dwarven realm. That's you three. And Tali, of course."

"Why us? And how did you make this happen? And again, what do you get out of it?"

"Has this been the plan from the get-go?" asked Charles. "I'm impressed. Annoyed, and perplexed, which is not usual for me, but impressed nonetheless." He nodded to her with the respect he clearly felt was due.

"I'm not impressed."

"Neither am I," growled Shi. "Couldn't you have just helped your great-nephew out of the goodness of your heart?"

"I did. Whatever resources were available to me, I put at your disposal. Didn't I source the dragon's egg for Charles all those years ago in the hopes we could infiltrate the elves' home?"

"Yes, you did," admitted Shi.

"And I told you both I would do whatever I could to help. But Charles insisted it was his plan to run. But I helped to try to get the attention of the elves, and that fool, Eleron, and we did. I offered many times, but when the time came, all I could do was send the horses for you as we couldn't risk Eleron becoming suspicious."

"But?" asked Charles.

"Ever since this plan was formed, I knew there could be more to it. That once you were re-united as a family, you would be an invincible team. With Charles' intelligence, his ability to unravel problems and solve them, and with Shi's fighting skills and Kifo's fearlessness, not to mention Tali, I knew you could go on to greater things. And I was right."

"Eloise, I swear to god, if you don't just get to the point..." sighed Charles, exasperated.

"Don't you dare!" she warned, her face dark, her magic gathering as the air cooled and grew heavy before lifting as she let herself relax. "Like it or not, I am the matriarch of this family and I will have respect. You younger ones may not believe it, especially you, Kifo, but I have ensured your survival over these years and will continue to do so. You may not agree with what I stand for, how I go about my business, but I have you, and all Necros, foremost in my mind whatever I do. So watch your mouth, and remember to whom you speak."

"What was the plan, then?" I asked.

"Did Rhyadid give you more information about the crown?"

Charles nodded. He reached into his jacket pocket and removed the small silver orb. "She gave me this. We were told it had the relevant information. Why is this so important to you, Eloise?"

"Charles, and all of you, don't you understand? You are the first group to ever enter and emerge from the elven homeworld. Ever. A few others have visited and returned, but none have ever remained as long as you. Dear Kifo and Tali even spent the night, if I am reading things correctly."

"We did."

"That is incredible! I can't wait to hear about it. And now you are off to meet dwarves. Again, only a handful of humans have ever visited. And I don't mean in the last few years. I mean ever. Don't you realize how incredible that is? What an achievement it is? I wanted to help, but I also want the information. I hope you are willing to go through a thorough debrief. And again when you return from the world of dwarves."

"I still don't get it," admitted Shi.

"Because it's important." Eloise leaned forward and placed several pieces of wood on the fire, focused on a delicate whisper as the flames caught and the smoke billowed, then sat ramrod straight and told us, "We need to know all we can about the other races. Information is nigh on impossible to get. You know more about the elves than any other human alive. That's incredible."

"We honestly didn't learn that much," I said.

"Nonsense. Surprise me. Tell me one thing you think I don't know about their world."

"Well, we did have an aerial battle with a man riding this weird beast. I called it a ceph. It had a blunt head and large wings, a thick, matte-gray hide, and they trained them but controlled them with something akin to whispers. I think it was for sport, but Rhyadid didn't seem to like it."

Eloise's eyes widened as she clapped her hands together and said, "Excellent. That's truly excellent. You see? Information. It is the ultimate power in this world and all others. You are in a privileged position. You have the permission of a powerful elf to venture into the dwarven world on a quest, no less. She gave you your life in exchange for this task, I presume?"

"She did," said Charles.

"Marvelous! Now we get to learn about the dwarves. We will study the orb closely and see what information she has given you. Even this is invaluable. We have next to zero knowledge of the dwarves. Less than the elves. We need to know. With you there, we will have more information than all Necros have managed to obtain in our entire history."

"But for what purpose?" I asked yet again.

"We are part of this thing called the Necroverse," said Eloise patiently. "Yet other races know more about us than we do about them. That isn't fair. It leaves us at a great disadvantage. Information is power. Knowledge is mightier than the sword. I wish to know because I feel it is important for the future of our entire kind. The more we understand of the other races, the better position we are in to deal with them. Make alliances, forge friendships, help them, and hopefully they will help us."

"That's it?" I asked. "Nothing else? Just information?"

"Yes, just information so we can ensure our own survival. Things are stirring in the Necroverse. Change is coming, I can feel it. Maybe not for centuries, or even millennia, but the universe is in a constant state of flux. Once dwarves and elves were best friends. Maybe they will be again. We need to know these things. We need contact with them. We need to learn as much about them as they know about us. This is a small, almost insignificant start, but at least it is a start. I shall return once you have rested to see what the orb contains, but for now I shall leave you in peace. Sleep, eat, recover. And well done."

Eloise stood, then she was gone.

The fire roared. Smoke spread through the compound, sending us into a coughing fit.

"Drama much?" spluttered Shi.

The smoke gradually cleared and we remained seated, watching the flames until the silence was absolute.

"Are you going to say it, or shall I?" I asked.

"There's no need," sighed Charles, rubbing at his face.

"There is," said Shi.

"She's playing us, right?" I said. "She's up to something, and she wants more than just information."

"Undoubtedly," said Charles, staring at the silver orb resting in his palm.

"What?" I asked.

"I guess we'll find out once we visit the dwarves and recover this crown."

"You aren't serious?" said Shi, absentmindedly picking up his sword as if the next battle was about to begin.

"We don't have a choice," said Charles. "Eloise is the least of our worries. Rhyadid said if we did this then the slate's wiped clean. We retrieve the crown, she opens a portal and we send it through, and that's the end of our involvement with the elves. No more portals, no unexpected visits from Eleron, and we can get on with the rest of our lives."

"And you trust her?" I asked.

Charles pocketed the orb and looked at us both. "There are two people, and two people only, who I trust in this world or any other, and I am sitting with them right now. No, I do not trust Eloise, or Rhyadid, or anyone else. We are blood brothers. Bonded in battle and intrigue. Three generations of Necro men who will always look out for one another. We have no choice in this, but that doesn't mean we have to like it."

"Or let Eloise treat us like playthings," I said.

"There's one thing you should know about her, Kifo," said Charles. "Whatever she tells you, there is always more to it. Who knows what she really wants out of this? Right now, it doesn't even matter. We do what we must, and we survive."

"We survive," I agreed.

"So we're really doing this?" asked Shi.

"We're going to infiltrate the dwarven realm to recover a crown for an elf queen," I laughed. "This is crazy."

"But fun," said Charles with a smile.

"Yeah, it is," I admitted. "More cake?"

THE END

The next book in the series is **Dwarven Madness**. Pick up your copy now and continue the adventure.

Our Little Chat

Thanks for reading! As an independent full-time author, reviews are always important. If you could spare a moment to leave a review before checking out the next book, I would really appreciate it. It helps boost visibility for the series, which generates sales. That means I can write more about dragons and the Necroverse.

This series is part of the broader Necroverse. Shi makes several brief guest appearances in Notes of Necrosoph, and Eleron causes untold problems, although you do not need to read one series to enjoy the other. Obviously, I'd love it if you did read them both. There's a dragon, and we get to watch him grow from a baby wyrmling over time. Please check it out if you haven't already done so, but don't forget to continue this series and pick up a copy of Dwarven Madness.

Stay jiggy,

Al